Rise Of Mankind Book 1

John Walker

DISCLAIMER

This is a work of fiction. Names, characters, business, places, events, and incidents are either the products of the author's imagination or used in a fictitious manner. Any resemblance to actual persons, living or dead, or actual events is purely coincidental. This story contains explicit language and violence.

Blurb

Three years ago, Earth was attacked by an invading force so devastating, only one ship in the fleet survived. Their hard won victory came from the aid of an alliance of aliens long at war with an aggressive force. With the aid of advanced technology, humanity retrofitted their surviving vessel. The Behemoth became a shield against any future incursions.

Now a strange ship has arrived, heading straight toward Earth. As it is not answering hails, the Behemoth heads out to intercept. The operation is interrupted by other visitors from beyond the solar system. Outnumbered the Behemoth must fend off the invaders once again but this time, the stakes are much higher.

Chapter 1

Something pulsed. A quick interruption in the endless hum collected by long range scanners directed at the edge of the solar system. Lieutenant Oliver Darnell caught it immediately and brought up a list of operations in the area. Increased mining work might account for a false positive on the early warning system.

But the schedule showed no civilian activity in that particular region. Olly frowned and redirected the necessary resources to gather more data. The hair on the back of his neck bristled as he thought of the last time such an anomaly occurred. Three years ago, Earth lacked the technology to proactively detect an incursion so far out. Signs of the attack were studied after the fact and catalogued for future reference.

Olly busied himself preparing analytical applications, programs designed to capture as much data as possible on the second ping. He adjusted his headphones for better noise cancellation, cutting out his fellow crew members as they went about their tasks.

Boosting the gain, he stared at the screen intently, willing it to hurry up.

Enhanced long range equipment combined with high speed satellite relays made his job a lot easier. When he graduated from the academy, the system hadn't been fully deployed. Data mining took hours back then but with a little help from the Alliance and some human creativity, Olly could monitor the Solar System in close to real time.

The second pulse made Olly's heart race. He hoped it might be a glitch in the sensor arrays but no. Something was definitely out there moving fast. His analytics went into action, plotting speed and course, method of propulsion all while trying to capture the shape of the object.

These initial tests would rule out whether Olly found something natural like a comet or space debris and tell him whether it came from one of the friendly cultures of the Alliance or...the other guys.

A tap on his shoulder made Olly jump and he turned to see Lieutenant Commander Stephanie Redding smirking at him. She was a fit woman in her early forties, her dusty blond hair thick on the top and cropped short at the bottom. Her service record spoke of a brilliant pilot and her extensive experience also made her a logical third in command.

Olly pulled the headphones away from his ears and sat up straight. "I'm sorry, Ma'am."

"What's got you so intent?" Redding tilted her head to see his screen. "What're you tracking there?"

"I'm not entirely sure yet." He let out a breath and turned back to the data. "I hope to have a report ready soon. Whatever it is seems to have appeared near Pluto."

"Conventional travel?" Redding asked. Olly anticipated the question but he didn't have a good answer.

"Our early warning doesn't go beyond our solar system so it's possible the thing has been trundling along at sub-light."

"Opinion?"

Olly shrugged. "Do you want pessimism?"

"I'll take realistic."

"Okay, let's take a stab at this." Olly put his readings on the main screen, a bunch of charts and constantly flickering numbers off to the right. "What we're looking at here is trajectory and velocity. Right now, it's moving in a consistent direction. This column here shows how it's defying gravitational pulls of larger items it passes."

"Like a space craft."

Olly nodded. "Exactly. I'm analyzing its propulsion now…" He tapped away at the keyboard, frowning at what he discovered. "I see thrust and fluctuating power output consistent with the amount of energy necessary to defy those solar bodies but something is preventing me from penetrating the hull."

"Could it be Alliance?" Redding squinted at the screen. "A message?"

Olly let out a long breath. "Sure. Or…"

"I know what you're going to say, Lieutenant." Redding hummed. "You said it's moving in a consistent direction. Give me the course heading."

"Here, Ma'am," Olly replied. "It's heading for Earth."

Redding stood up straighter and moved back to her station. "Ensign," she directed her comment to the communications officer, Agatha White, one of the newest additions to the bridge crew. She'd only just graduated from the academy and through stunning marks, got a post on the Behemoth. Olly liked her but at only twenty years old, the girl proved a little naive for his taste. "Patch me through to Commander Everly."

"Aye, Ma'am." Agatha turned to her console and worked the controls.

Redding continued, "keep compiling information, Olly. Whatever that thing is, I kind of doubt anyone invited it. The captain will want a serious briefing. Make sure you have everything he needs."

"Aye, Ma'am." Olly put his headphones back on and hunkered down. All the times he complained about the boredom of third watch came back to haunt him. If this thing heralded another attack, would the Behemoth be able to hold them back? And what if they'd found something else even more terrifying than the bastards who attacked them before?

He shook his head and forced himself to focus. Idle thinking would do no one any good. Gathering facts, compiling data and providing these reports would go much further than speculation or fear. Humanity had lived in the shadow of terror for too long. They'd bounced back from devastation once already. Oliver wanted to believe they never would have to again.

But the Behemoth had not been truly tested yet, not against a real foe. Conventional weapons no longer proved a match for the vessel, but what of the advanced armaments of their true enemy? Even the Alliance officer couldn't say for sure and she came with a lot of experience.

Perhaps this object would be the maiden voyage the Behemoth needed to prove not only to her crew but the people of Sol as well that they had a real deterrent against interstellar marauders. All the cultures of the world got behind the rebuilding of the Behemoth and many hopes were pinned on her success.

I sure hope she's up to the challenge, Olly thought as a third wave of information filled his screen. *The best equipment and resources money can buy went into this beast. Us humans are probably the weakest link. Here's to hoping we're up to the pressure...and whatever this thing represents. Okay, Darnell. Parse this data and get to work. The time for wonder is over.*

***

Captain Gray Atwell smirked at the intent expression of Clea An'Tufal as she puzzled over the chessboard, carefully contemplating every piece. He'd learned a lot about the alien in three years of working with her. The liquid silver irises and black-purple hair provided the outward signs of how she differed from humans, but those were merely superficial. To understand the differences of a Kielan, one had to delve into their culture.

Gray found it easiest to compare them to the Japanese with their stringent discipline and impressive work ethic. Kielans seemed to take it to an extreme. Clea worked harder than any three human technicians, tirelessly moving from one shift to the next as one part advisor, one part worker. She learned swiftly and adapted to situations exceedingly well.

Best of all, during grueling hours of work, she maintained a good sense of humor. He'd never seen her succumb to misery. Yes, she sacrificed some dizzying emotional highs by not experiencing the lows but Gray considered it a pretty fair trade. She'd explained once that the concept of depression was foreign to them. They'd defeated the state of mind centuries ago.

Kielans boasted many traits which made them enviable but their culture wasn't perfect. They suffered under the weight of familial expectation and most children followed in the footsteps of their parents. This meant they always had someone to live up to, someone who's successes and contributions to society may have been very high.

Clea said she volunteered to be the liaison for Earth because such work tended to be difficult to compare to others. She had a better chance of being judged on her own merits than those of the people who came before her. Gray understood. He chose to join the military rather than follow in his father's footsteps into the world of application programming.

As a result, no one would compare him to his father in anything but morality and personal accountability.

The fact an alien race which evolved thousands of light years from Earth fostered the same desire to be measured individually fascinated Gray. Clea started out as someone he wanted to understand and eventually became a friend. Despite their differences, and often because of them, they complimented each other well in the preparations of the Behemoth as a bleeding edge military vessel.

"You know, you're never going to win if you just stare at them," Gray teased and took a sip of brandy. "I'm pretty sure you already know how you're going to beat me anyway."

"I've played through this game six times, Gray," Clea replied evenly. "Right now, there are one hundred ninety-seven thousand seven-hundred forty-two possible games we could experience."

"Please tell me you're not planning on going through them all in your head right now," Gray said. "And where did you pull that number out of? Some kind of computational craziness?"

"No." Clea glanced up at him, smirking. "I read it on the extranet the other day. Apparently, there are almost infinite possibilities when it comes to chess. The article stated a typical session takes about forty moves with an average of thirty choices per move. Shocking for a seemingly simple pass time with only thirty-two pieces, wouldn't you say?"

"Those are some pretty insane statistics." Gray scratched at the white hair of his right temple. Five short years ago, his hair was nearly black but the attack and then years of feverishly administering the rebuilding of the Behemoth took a toll on him. He remained fit but his hair betrayed his age and at nearly fifty, he sometimes felt it.

His blue eyes carried wisdom and all the difficult decisions he made over the past twenty-five years as a military officer. He remained lean, his powerful frame still muscular and fit. Aches and pains hadn't really set in but a few exercise sessions reminded him he was no longer twenty-five years old.

Even modern medical technology, which kept people going for vastly longer than a hundred years before, couldn't take away the weight of the spirit. Gray saw a great deal during his military career and he carried those experiences everywhere he went.

"Don't worry, Captain," Clea said, moving her pawn two paces. "I'm pretty sure you've got a good chance at winning this time."

"Why?" Gray leaned forward and took her pawn with his. "Am I due?"

"In a word, yes." Clea shrugged. "Either that or you're getting what you deserve for all those times you trounced me while I was still learning."

"As we both know, sometimes the best way to learn is to lose." Gray glanced out the porthole at the stars beyond and let out a deep breath. "The key is to ensure your losses don't carry costs too high to make the knowledge worth it."

Clea clicked her tongue, a behavior she learned from the Chief Engineer Higgins. "You're drifting back to the attack, Gray."

Gray held up his hands. "I didn't say anything at all! *You* brought it up."

"Really." Clea raised her brows. "Humans can be very coy when they want to be. How do you do it? Pretend as if you're not thinking of something when it's quite obvious you are?"

"Self-deception?" Gray grinned. "We're the *masters* at that."

"Oh yes, I'm *quite* aware." Clea didn't look at the board as she moved another piece. "Check."

Gray squinted at the game. Just as he reached to make his move, the com buzzed. *Saved by the bell,* he mused to himself, *I hope*. He moved over to his desk and engaged the connection. "Captain Atwell here."

"Gray, it's Adam." Commander Adam Everly was his first officer and oldest friend. They'd attended the academy together though graduated a year apart. Since then, they served at many of the same posts. "Redding contacted me from the bridge. They picked something up on long range scans. They want us to see the data right away."

Gray's heart leaped in his chest. Could this be the precursor to another attack? Three years ago, Earth scientists retrospectively examined data collected from the borders of their solar system. Their findings led to the construction of the satellite array positioned near every planet and solar body with a predictable gravitational rotation.

Are they back?

Gray turned to Clea who stared back at him with a grave expression. They both knew it was possible. They may well be on the verge of another skirmish, one without the benefit of Alliance intervention. But he knew enough not to jump to conclusions. He needed to shake off his worry. The crew would pick up on it immediately. Calm confidence settled over him, the exact sensation he needed his people to see in the face of the unknown.

"Thanks Adam," Gray replied. "Clea and I will meet you in the briefing room. Have Olly bring his findings."

"Sure thing. See you there." The connection cleared.

"I guess our game's on pause." Gray pulled on his uniform jacket, black with gold piping on the shoulders and seams. He fastened the silver buttons up the front and straightened his collar. "Shall we?"

"Indeed." Clea donned her own coat, a mirror of the captain's with fewer bars on the shoulder. As a liaison, she enjoyed the rank of Lieutenant Commander but tended to exert her authority only when absolutely necessary. "It may not be what you think."

"Then again," Gray headed into the hall before continuing, "it very well might be. Do you know any Latin?"

"I'm afraid not."

"*Si vis pacem, para bellum*," Gray said. "It's something my military history professor spouted off like a prayer. I always thought he was just being pretentious but when the attack came, his words came back to haunt me and I agree with them more than ever before. If we'd followed them then, we might've stood more of a chance."

"So what does it mean?"

"*If you want peace, prepare for war*," Gray replied. He looked around as they walked, admiring the solid design all around him. Thick metal coated the walls, screens here and there displayed readings from various departments throughout the vessel. He felt it hum beneath his feet like a sailing ship of old succumbing to the waves. "I think the Behemoth fits the saying, don't you?"

"If anything could embody the concept of preparing for war, this machine would be it," Clea agreed. "My human history is nothing compared to yours but there is one thing I picked up in my reading."

"Oh?" Gray summoned the elevator. "Do tell."

"Humans have many talents. You are all infinitely creative and cunning, capable of amazing feats when your backs are pressed to the wall. And in those days when your enemies gather around you and threaten what you hold dear, you fight with a ferocity my kind has only seen in the very threat we all face now."

"Oh, I don't know, Clea. Every living thing wants to live. Self-preservation compels us all."

"Not to the same extent as humanity exhibits." They boarded the elevator. "At least, that's if your history books are to be believed and are not merely fiction. After all, the battle of Thermopylae suggests some pretty outlandish behavior. How much of that do you feel is mere boasting?"

"I don't know but I will tell you this. The Greeks of that era knew what was at stake when the Persians came to their doorstep. The total annihilation of their way of life. If those three hundred Spartans would not have given the rest of Greece time to rally, Western thinking may never have come to be. I can relate to the generals of that time right now...facing an overwhelming foe with so few but like them, we have an advantage."

"Which is?"

"We want it more, Clea. We want to win...to hold on to our way of life and the freedoms we enjoy and no one, not a foreign fleet of zealots or any other unknown horror out of space will take it away from us."

"Desire alone does not win a battle, Captain."

"No...but without it, you're guaranteed to lose a war."

Chapter 2

Everything always happens on third or fourth shift. Adam pinged the various department leads, hastily putting together a briefing. *I can't remember the last eventful midday shift*. Indeed, the crew of the Behemoth spent most of its time training with the new equipment. They weren't even part of the police patrol roster. Day after day, they maintained lunar orbit and prepared for a day which may never come.

Better safe than sorry I guess. Adam believed they spent their time wisely but quietly, he itched to be *doing* something. Earth admins played cautiously, praying humanity might drum up enough rare minerals to finish the construction of a second Behemoth but they were years away from a functional vessel.

We should hook up with the Alliance and take the fight to the enemy. Adam smiled to himself as he considered what his professors at the academy would've said about his opinion. They considered him a brilliant but impulsive battlefield commander. He excelled in desperate situations, the kind he tended to get himself into. While he generally won his mock engagements, the few he lost tended to be...well...bad.

Besides, even though he wanted to contribute to whatever fight raged beyond the borders of their solar system, he recognized the importance of staying put. After all, nothing could defend the Earth like the Behemoth and nothing would for the foreseeable future. The duty might feel boring but sometimes the least exciting task proved to be the most important.

The briefing room represented one of the major advancements to come from the Alliance. A shiny, metallic table occupied the center of the room with fiber cushioned chairs flanking it on either side. Each station boasted a detachable tablet which controlled the nanofilament screens which made up the walls. Whoever made their presentation could display their information wherever it was most convenient.

Gathering department heads tended to be easier said than done. The Behemoth proved to be the largest military asset ever built. Even before the repairs and upgrade, she represented the pinnacle of human ingenuity and creative design. The name came honestly and, much like her cousins the naval aircraft carriers, she represented a small city worth of personnel, activity and problems.

Many of the support staff on board were raw and untested but their leadership was drawn from some of the most experienced veterans the Earth could muster. Many junior officers appreciated the opportunity this afforded them, to learn and train alongside the best military minds of the current age. Adam felt no small relief about his team, especially if they were expected to fend off a potentially overwhelming foe.

They'd need all the help they could get.

The Behemoth housed nine squadrons of fighter crafts of various types. Interceptors, bombers and reconnaissance craft made up the bulk of their contingency. Repair facilities were spread between four distinct hangars. If an attack damaged one, they would still be seventy-five percent combat effective.

One hundred-twenty pilots supported daily operations from patrols to combat maneuvers. Each trained with the advanced technology prevalent in their respective ships and they cross trained in basic repairs and maintenance. On downtime, these men and women would be able to get their own ships back into space in the event of a serious engagement.

Everyone aboard followed this same protocol. They mastered their own job then learned another. Deficits due to illness, injury or death could be handled by a backup. The large crew made this possible, even practical considering the varied nature of assignments and requirements to keep the ship going.

Group Commander Estaban Revente oversaw the contingency of fighter pilots aboard. He flew hundreds of sorties during some of the worst national conflicts, making him a man of extensive experience. A brash flyer at the beginning of his career, a solid record gave his subordinates something to look up to.

Even though some of his antics came back to haunt him from time to time. It was hard to discipline a junior when they were trying something he came up with a decade before. Still, coming from a place of *been there, survived it* gave him credibility a less seasoned soldier would lack.

Lieutenant Colonel Marshall Dupont commanded the marine security forces aboard. His unit consisted of a full contingent of security personnel for ship side order, two special forces platoons and a large ground force capable of heavy operations. As a field soldier, he tended to be fairly reserved in regards to day to day events but when they called upon him, he made it clear he expected to have operational command of any ground based mission.

Adam believed in the guy. They hadn't served together but Marshall's record spoke for itself. He'd chewed a lot of dirt in his day and provided leadership in some of the most intense environments known to man. During a terrorist hostage situation in an orbiting research facility, he restored order to an impossible situation in four days. When he joined the Behemoth crew, a lot of minds were put at ease to have such extensive experience.

Lieutenant Commander Maury Higgins acted as chief engineer for the Behemoth and had been on board even before the attack. He knew the ship better than anyone alive, including the designers. As the man in charge of all mechanical operations, he tended to be a strict task master but his men considered him fair. If he had an opportunity for improvement, it would be his high, bordering on unfair expectations.

People had a lot to live up to under Maury's command and as a result, some of the best and brightest young technicians kept the Behemoth running.

Lieutenant Commander Laura Brand filled the chief medical officer role. Two separate hospitals occupied the vessel, another redundancy in the event of catastrophic damage. Each high capacity area provided plenty of space for a lot of casualties. Both fell under Brand's supervision.

The Behemoth was Laura's first ship assignment. Prior to that, she operated the Lunar space station's medical wing and taught at the academy. When the opportunity arose to join the ship's crew, she did so grudgingly but considering many of the people under her command came from the ranks of her students, she felt a need to be involved. Few supervisors would know their people as well as she did and as their manager, she could play to their strengths.

Lieutenant Commander Redding and Lieutenant Darnell arrived before the others, the latter carrying a tablet, looking nervous. Adam waved them over and lowered his voice, glancing at the door to ensure they were alone.

"Olly, just deliver the facts during this briefing," Adam patted the younger man's shoulder. "No speculation unless you're asked to, got it?"

"Sir, I fully understand," Olly replied, "but I'm not sure—"

"I'm talking about your uncanny ability to guess. Sometimes, you're spot on but in this case, stick to what we know. There'll be a lot of experience in this room. Let them throw out the theories and you can help us build them up or tear them down."

Olly nodded. "Yes, sir."

"Redding," Adam turned his attention to the pilot, "I trust you've had navigation plot an intercept course for timing."

Redding nodded. "Yes, sir. Tim worked with Olly and we could be there in five hours at full speed. Less if we engaged the hyperjump."

"Wow, it's really hauling." Adam wanted to ask more questions but people began to fill the room, taking their seats. The captain had yet to arrive but when he did, they'd be expected to dive right away. "Party's about to start. Take your seats."

Adam sat down and observed the others. Their expressions spoke of worry, fear, excitement and curiosity. No one had any illusions. *Something* would've come around eventually. If not the enemy or the Alliance, they knew other cultures, other beings existed out there in the galaxy. Eventually, Earth would no longer be some distant place ignored by universal civilizations.

Surviving an attack from an overwhelming enemy counted for something.

Captain Atwell and Clea entered the room at a brisk pace and everyone stood at attention. Adam watched them take their positions beside their chairs before Gray nodded at his leadership team. "At ease and please be seated."

After they settled, Gray turned to Adam. "Go ahead."

"At twenty-two sixteen, Lieutenant Darnell picked up a blip on the edge of the solar system while monitoring long range scans and early warning systems." Adam tapped at his tablet for a moment and brought up a map of the solar system. It appeared near Pluto. "This is where it was when we discovered it. As you can see, it's traveling at point five light speed."

Maury spoke up, "which means it can reach earth in roughly ten hours...unless it accelerates."

"Readings show it has not increased speed since entering our solar system," Olly said.

Gray stared at the screen for a moment before speaking. "Give us a break down on your data. What do we know about this thing?"

Olly stood and used his tablet to display information on all the screens. "It's definitely a ship measuring at fifteen-hundred, twenty-four meters. The signature matches no known ships in the Alliance database and I haven't been able to determine hull material or density."

"Fifteen-hundred meters..." Maury shook his head, eyes wide. "It's got us beat by over a hundred and fifty meters! How're you not able to gather data on the material makeup?"

"Like us, they utilize an operating shield but theirs goes beyond protecting them from casual debris." Olly brought up a series of figures and math. "Somehow, it deflects deep scans. I've used every trick I can think of but can't get through. If we got closer, I might be able to penetrate it but for now, anything within the shield is a mystery."

"Any guesses at offensive capabilities?" Estaban asked. "Obvious weapons or even radioactive leakage?"

"No, sir," Olly said. "Here's the signature of the vessel." An almond shaped object appeared. Four holes in the back provided forward propulsion. The perfectly smooth surface lacked any noticeable windows or bulges which might be weapons. The pointed front end looked sharp. It reminded Adam of a sword fish.

"So we have no idea who it is," Gray said, "or what they want. Only that they're on a course for Earth and moving pretty damn fast. How long before we could intercept?"

"At their current speed, roughly five hours," Adam replied. "Less if we enter a hyperjump."

Gray shook his head. "I'm not keen on testing our hyperdrive just on the verge of first contact. Assuming they're currently operating at full speed, it means we're evenly matched in the propulsion department. Opinions anyone?"

"I'd recommend we initiate Ready Thirty for all crews," Estaban said. "If this thing turns hostile, we'll want our people out there fast. When it gets closer, I'd increase to Ready Five."

Gray nodded. "Agreed. Anyone else?"

"What're the chances of this being a diplomatic vessel?" Laura asked. "Signs of aggression might be taken poorly."

"They're not making any intentions clear," Adam replied. "Good, bad or indifferent. For all we know, it might be a ghost ship."

"Or a fire ship," Maury muttered.

"What's that, Maury?" Gray turned to him.

"Like in the wooden ship days," Maury continued. "They'd catch one of their fast moving crafts on fire and set it on a collision course with a blockade or port. It caused plenty of chaos back then and this thing, flying straight for Earth? If it doesn't slow down…"

"It would be like a super meteor," Olly finished the sentence.

The thought brought some unrest to the room but Gray lifted a hand. "Let's not jump to conclusions about light speed super missiles. Marshall, what if we have to board the thing? How long would it take to clear?"

"Without knowing their defensive capabilities," Marshall said, "and going on sheer size alone, it could take a while. Days without good intel, maybe more. It's the size of a small city when it comes to the decks and all the crannies we'd have to search and that's assuming our opponents would fight directly. We might be stuck in a guerrilla battle on someone else's home turf."

"Understood." Gray nodded. "Are your men prepared for such a...well, nightmare?"

"As much as they can be," Marshall replied. "I'd insist on gathering more intelligence. Anything would help and nothing...well, if we come away with a total unknown, then we're risking a lot of lives."

"Got it." Gray turned to Clea. "What do you think? You've been pretty quiet over there."

"The enemy has yet to send a ship like this against any Alliance planet that I'm aware of." Clea tilted her head, studying the signature. "Unfortunately, without more data everything we come up with will be conjecture."

"Do you think it's one of your people?" Adam asked. "An Alliance ship of some kind?"

"It's possible," Clea nodded. "They may have built something like it since I've been here. News does travel rather slowly but I somehow doubt it. This may well be something completely new. But again, without being there, I'm just guessing."

"Alright," Gray said, standing up. "Let's get out there and investigate. Adam, order the alert thirty. Redding, have navigation plot an intercept course just ahead of our guest and engage full speed. Everyone else, prepare your departments for a fight. If they're peaceful, it won't be a hardship to shut down the gun batteries but if not...well, I won't get caught with my pants down."

"Quite the vulgar term, Captain," Clea said.

Gray grinned. "Not as bad as it could be. You have your orders everyone. Send your ready reports to the bridge. I want everyone on operational standby in less than thirty minutes. Dismissed."

That's why Adam liked Gray and why he accepted the post on the Behemoth. The man knew how to be prepared. He erred on the side of caution and gave history the value it deserved. When some unidentified ship came crashing into their solar system before, they weren't ready. In some ways, they still weren't. Many systems had yet to be fully tested and the crew itself never fought with the tools at their disposal.

But Gray would ensure they had every advantage available. The Behemoth may not be a seasoned veteran of many battles since its Christening but she sure came a long way since surviving the attack. Everyone on board knew the stakes of another fight with the enemy and all of them were as well trained as any soldier hoped to be.

Their maiden operation may well be against some unknown threat but that just gave the mission a higher value. No one learned from the easy stuff. Mankind needed challenges to grow. Adam wondered just how great an opportunity this thing presented. He looked forward to seeing his people in action either way.

The time for idleness was over.

Thank God.

Chapter 3

Gray and Clea stayed behind as the others left to prepare. She stood nearby, hands behind her back as she watched him request a connection to Commodore Billings. While the screen flickered, he turned his attention to the woman and shrugged, inviting her to speak before prompting.

"Okay, what's on your mind?"

"I assume you're contacting high command to inform them of what we're about to do."

Gray nodded. "And?"

"They can be...conservative with the use of this vessel," Clea replied. "Remember when they denied your request to intervene with the pirates hitting the mining operations out near Neptune?"

"Yes, but that was different," Gray said, "and I agreed with them. The pirates returned to their little base off the coast of Africa and conventional forces apprehended them. Whatever's out there, that's our job. They're going to let us deal with it."

"Providing we're the ones to deal with it." Clea gestured to the terminal. "I have no complaints."

Gray started to reply but paused as the call connected. "Meet me on the bridge. We'll talk more soon."

Gray got used to her silver eyes years before but occasionally, she could stare at him with such an odd expression, it reminded him of her origin. As human as she behaved, as much as they wore off on her, she still came from a very different place and when she felt a conversation had not ended, she made it clear with her unique scowl.

She spun on her heel and left without another word. He figured they'd definitely pick *that* conversation up later.

Commodore Billings appeared on the screen, sitting at his posh desk in the Miami headquarters. Palm trees swayed out the window behind him and beyond those, the white caps covered the sea. Clea's opinion of high command came from their surroundings. Their tropical paradise location made it hard to take their opinion too seriously. After all, how much could they really know about hot situations?

"What can I do for you, Gray?"

"Thanks for taking the call, Sam," Gray sat down. "I'm sending you a report we picked up on long range scanners. You can read it if you want but we don't have a lot of time. A large object, possibly a ship, has entered our solar system. It's on a direct course for Earth. It'll be here in less than ten hours."

Sam's expression turned grave. "I see what you're talking about. Does your team have any idea what it is?"

Gray shook his head. "Not yet, but we intend to find out. We're prepping to intercept."

Billings narrowed his eyes. "Do you believe this might be another attack?"

"I don't want to speculate. Could be anything but one thing I do know is it's bigger than us and just as fast. Clea didn't recognize the design and we have no matches on any database."

"Understood." Billings sighed. "Listen, Gray. I can't authorize you to take the Behemoth that far away from Earth. Not when this could be...well, it could be anything. A ruse for another attack for example. You're the only thing keeping this place safe."

"Sam, it's coming here. Would you rather me let it get to our backyard?"

"If you're five hours away from here with only an untested hyperjump as your method of return, what good are you going to be doing us? No. You need to stay close.'

Gray sighed, looking away. "We're at least going to break orbit and meet it in open space, far enough away from inhabited areas to avoid any damage."

"That I *can* authorize. Just remember, you're our shield, Gray. Not an arrow."

"We really have to consider the future," Gray said. "You may not think so now, but eventually this ship's going to have to go abroad."

"It's not that we don't trust you, but you should understand our caution. We're in the midst of building another ship and when we do, we'll have the luxury of traveling around the solar system. Right now, the conventional fleet can handle internal security. Your purpose is to *protect*. Is that clear?"

Gray nodded, doing his best not to look away. "Perfectly."

"Just...be careful with this thing. We can't afford to lose you guys. It would really trash morale."

Gray chuckled. "That'll be our biggest concern. I'll keep you up to date on what we find. We'll break orbit shortly and get into position...shield you guys from whatever this is."

"Sounds good."

"Hey, don't forget to wear sun screen before you hit that beach." Gray tried to lighten the mood. "I don't think you can afford a serious sunburn."

"Don't give me a hard time about this post. You know I'm from Alaska. This tropical heat's killing me."

"Yeah," Gray shook his head. "Things are tough all over, buddy. Behemoth out."

***

Captain Atwell took his seat on the bridge as Adam prepped the bridge for departure. Ensign Agatha White worked with orbital command to clear the area. Various civilian and police vessels crowded Lunar space as people went about their daily activities. The academy contributed to the majority of this congestion and Gray knew they practiced fleet maneuvers during every shift.

Weapon tests near the moon made sense and that's why the Behemoth berthed there.

"Commander," Agatha turned in her seat to address the room, "space lanes are cleared. We are free to depart for the next thirty minutes."

"You heard her, Redding," Adam said. "Initiate protective field and get us underway. Thrusters only. Let's keep this as clean as possible."

"Aye, sir." Redding turned to the navigator, Tim Collins. "Give me a guide to open space please."

Tim ran his fingers along the smooth console, his eyes flitting left and right as he performed his tasks. "It's…up now."

Redding nodded. "Got it. Protective field engaged. Thrusters are…active. ETA to open space, five minutes."

"Give us plenty of room to engage the pulse engines," Adam said. "Let's not mess up school maneuvers with a sub-light wake."

"Academy vessels are well outside of our range, sir," Olly announced. "They'll for sure see us though."

Gray grinned. What he wouldn't have given as a young cadet to see a war vessel like the Behemoth leave dock. He imagined the distraction and the instructors cursing about it before reprimanding their students back to the task at hand. Hopefully, if all went as planned those young men and women would pilot a sister ship to the Behemoth. A little excitement might go a long way toward improving morale.

Might not be a victory but we take what we can get.

Far off in the bowels of the ship, the pulse reactor fired up. Containment kept the ship from vibrating but the raw power fired up his soul, giving him a brief adrenalized rush of excitement. They participated in only a few police engagements since entering active duty but nothing compared to embarking on a real mission, one with unknown variables and real danger.

Clea took the seat to his left. Adam sat on the right. She watched the view port impassively, legs crossed with her hands resting on her knee. Gray wondered what she thought of the mission and whether or not getting into action fired up her blood. Kielans seemed to be reserved by nature but their chess games occasionally annoyed her out of her disciplined shell. They weren't emotionless, just controlled.

"We have cleared Lunar orbit," Redding announced. "Heading into deep space. ETA three minutes, twenty-five seconds."

"Steady as she goes," Adam replied. "Olly, are we still clear on scans?"

"Aye, sir," Olly said. "There's no way anyone wants to get in our way but we do have an audience."

Adam smirked. "Try not to wave at them as you go by, Redding."

"The thought never crossed my mind, sir." Redding chuckled. "But there was that time..."

"Yes, we all know," Tim interrupted. "And I don't think anyone wants to hear about it again."

"It was only garbage," Redding replied. "Not like I made them dump a cargo full of medical supplies or anything."

"Let's focus on the task at hand, people," Adam said. "Past glories...or otherwise...can wait for the mess hall."

Gray leaned toward Clea, keeping his voice down. "What're you thinking about?"

"Working through the variables," Clea replied. "Since we have no idea what we're walking into, I figured I'd at least contemplate the problem. Maybe I'll think of questions we'll need to ask."

"Are you leaning toward anything? Any theories at all?"

Clea nodded. "A few but they're meaningless. The weapon idea makes sense to me, mostly because if they were friendly, they would've communicated by now. With our satellites, we'd easily pick up any message they wanted to send. The fact they're running silent makes them all the more suspicious."

"True." Gray sighed. "They seem to be intent on Earth too, ignoring our outposts and mining operations."

"If they are an attack force, cutting off the head of the snake makes more sense than wasting time on outliers. However," Clea glanced in his direction, "they may not be counting on us. If their data is old, from before the attack, then we'll have a distinct advantage."

"What do you mean?"

"Undoubtedly their scans have shown them a massive warship standing guard. Watching Lieutenant Darnell's scans over there on monitor three, I've noticed they haven't deviated course nor made any sort of adjustment at all. For whatever reason, they don't care about us and that could mean they're unconcerned or uninformed. Either way, advantage."

"What would your military do in this situation?"

Clea drew a deep breath and let it out before replying. "We used to be a peaceful culture. One that would give anyone the benefit of the doubt. If a spaceship like that came to our doorstep, we'd send out diplomatic vessels and attempt to make contact. We wanted to share our technology and advancements with others. Suspicion came slowly to our minds."

"But now?" Gray prompted.

"Now, we're more like you. Assume the worst, hope for the best. I can't say we would've destroyed the thing outright but there is something to your saying *better to be safe than sorry*."

Gray nodded. His people may have developed the phrase but they only recently embraced it as totally as Clea suggested. In a little less than ten hours, they'd know the appropriate response.

He turned to his tablet and scanned reports from all sections. Each department reported ready for action well ahead of schedule. Third shift was about to end so they must've pulled in their relief. By the time the ship arrived, the next hands would be on staff and they'd be the ones to get them through their mission.

Gray made an adjustment to the schedules, cutting fourth shift short. This would ensure fresh bodies would be running things when the foreign vessel arrived. He'd address the ship and let them know what was happening and how he expected it to go down.

"We have cleared Lunar traffic," Redding announced. "Entering open space."

"Tim, plot a course to sector six-seven," Gray said.

"Course plotted, sir," Timothy said. "That's...roughly ten minutes away by pulse drive."

Clea turned to Gray. "We're not intercepting them?"

"We're the shield, not the arrow," Gray quoted. "We're going to meet them…just not all the way out there, away from our charge."

"They didn't give you authorization to leave." Clea clenched her fist.

"No, and I understand their reasons." Gray turned to Everly. "Get us into position. Darnell, keep your scans going and let me know if anything changes."

"Engage engines, Redding," Adam said.

"Aye sir." Redding got the ship moving.

"Ensign White," Gray said, "patch me through to ship wide communications."

"Aye, Captain." Agatha focused on her console for a moment before speaking. "You're live, sir."

"This is the captain speaking. So far, all we've really done involves training. Even the minor engagements we've seen are little more than stress tests on our hardware. As with most weapons like the Behemoth, sane people hope they never need to use them. Under rational situations, such a vessel would be called a deterrent.

I believe we all understood we could not be idle forever. There are threats still out there, cultures interested in our destruction and whether we are ready or not, they *will* descend upon us. It's not a matter of if, but when. Hope alone cannot hold back the tide. Our training and superior equipment, make us uniquely qualified to handle *any* threat the universe might throw our way.

I'm addressing you now because we have such a mission, something only we can meet. Lieutenant Darnell is sending out the report ship wide with our findings. Study it and understand what it means for your department. We're setting ourselves to Ready Thirty status. As we reach open space and wait for this object to arrive, security will lock down the corridors and leisure areas until the situation is resolved."

"Send any questions to your department leads. Let's get to work." Gray nodded to Agatha and she cut the line. "Alright people, we have a lot of time to stew on this situation. I want primary bridge crew to get a hot meal and sack time in the next hour. Darnell, keep up the scans with the time you have left then automate them. You need to be fresh when it arrives. Hopefully, we'll have plenty of answers soon."

"And perhaps more than we want," Clea muttered, "if we're to be honest."

"That's usually how it works," Gray replied. "Don't worry. I think we're nimble enough to handle whatever this thing throws at us."

Clea grinned. "Your confidence is almost infectious."

Gray laughed, shaking his head. "Just as your compliment is almost flattering."

Chapter 4

Nine Hours Later

Wing Commander Meagan Pointer wanted to itch her calf. It started ten minutes earlier and started driving her crazy. No amount of writhing around in the cockpit or concentration gave her relief. Whatever irritated her skin would continue to do so unhindered until she forgot about it, got killed or returned from her mission and ground her nails into her leg for a good ten minutes.

Ready Thirty status meant the flight teams needed to be capable of launching in thirty minutes from the moment the order was given. Her wing bunked out when they heard about the mission and by the time they were woken up by their CO, they were about to enter a Ready Five status.

They were roused an hour ahead of schedule, got cleaned up and headed down to the hangar. As the object drew closer, they each boarded their vessels, preparing to sit around in cramped space but no one knew what would happen when the foreign vessel arrived or if it would suddenly get their quicker.

This meant readiness despite comfort.

Meagan and her crew sat cooped up, combat ready for nearly an hour and a half. The complaints came as soon as Estaban gave them their briefing. Pilots hated waiting, especially on the verge of action. It was like putting a racing horse on the starting line, riling him up and then denying him the release of running. Maintaining combat intensity sure became hard when you sat still for so long.

Tactically, she understood the reason behind the heightened readiness. Combat situations tended to be fluid. Anything could happen at a moment's notice and, as a result, if fighters weren't poised to launch, they might not get out in a timely fashion. Every second in such an engagement was critical. The difference between victory and defeat might be spelled out in less than a minute.

Unfortunately, tactical readiness didn't allow for comfort. Hence her itching leg and Flight Lieutenant Manning's need to urinate.

A full spread of vessels were prepared to enter combat. Meagan's wing consisted of the FI-62 Interceptors, or Wasp, a highly maneuverable and fast ship. Armed with high intensity pulse lasers drawing power directly from their engine cores, slug throwing projectiles and guided missiles, they were a match for anything in its class. The advanced tech ensured weapon superiority, at least in their solar system.

Wings swept close to the body for tight maneuvers in space and extended for transatmospheric flight. Two turbine engines occupied the back with a number of thrusters all over the body for the type of movement only space allowed. Up, down, left and right gave a pilot great flexibility for dog fighting and they learned to think in three dimensions, to really use the technology to great advantage.

Inertial dampeners provided safety for the pilots by placing the cockpit at the center of a gyroscope.

Magnetics provided an appropriate reaction to quick maneuvers, reducing the massive G forces the Wasp pulled. This meant the difference between an operator tensing up and handling their ship effectively and…well…popping.

Training for those things was terrible and taxed the cadets almost as bad as special forces routines. They learned to take far worse than the ship's allowed so when they climbed into the first cockpit and familiarized themselves with reality, their tolerance far exceeded the requirements.

Flying the fighters still didn't cater to the faint of heart or out of shape but there wasn't a job in the system Meagan would rather have.

Wing Commander Rudy Hale sat at the head of the bomber group. Meagan attended the academy with him and he'd always preferred the heavier, lumbering ships to the quick ones every cadet had to master. At nearly six-feet tall and two hundred pounds, he defied the odds for being nearly too big to qualify for fighter duty. He believed his size meant he was destined to fly the biggest, most destructive crafts in the fleet.

The FB-15s, or Tiger Sharks, had a lot in common with their bigger, nearly forgotten ancestors, the B-52s. They operated on a crew of two, one for flying and the other taking on the dual task of navigation and weapons control. Each vessel carried ten warheads with more destructive power than five nuclear warheads from the twentieth century and those counted as conventional ordinance.

Pulse bombs, the real pride of modern weapon crafting, may well be the most destructive force humanity ever imagined. Under ideal conditions, test runs showed them capable of annihilating meteors roughly a quarter the size of Earth's moon. Dropping them at the perfect, precise location may be capable of exciting fault lines, causing seismic events throughout a region.

After shock from the pulse bombs facilitated heavy armor on the bombers, enough to deflect the EMP and secondary wave damage. Powerful engines and multi-point thrusters kept the ship steady though they'd still experience some serious turbulence. Because of these exceptional circumstances, bomber pilots attended an extra two weeks of training to familiarize themselves with the differences and required an additional one hundred hours of flight time to receive a certification.

These ships looked much like oversized Wasps with two additional turbines in the back but non-extending wings. They weren't designed for extreme maneuvers and so the designers didn't worry about the extremities becoming damaged under normal flight. Some of the best bombers handled their ships like they were in a smaller craft but they did so with real finesse.

One could easily over-fly a bomber, few knew how to push the limits without breaking them.

Her team held a distinguished code name, *Panther*. Another unit, long gone in a bygone age of early space travel, flew more than two hundred combat missions over the moon after the colonization. Those days involved so much lawlessness in space, it was a wonder the colonies survived and thanks to some pretty amazing pilots, they flourished.

They called Rudy's group the Bulls. He liked it but some of his juniors considered the name sexist. Considering how they barreled through any opposition and blew them back to hell, Meagan always thought it seemed fitting. Still, some people maintained sensitivity from civilian life. Most of them got over it eventually. Those who didn't, tended to be one tour types.

Meagan set her com to private and patched into her peer's cockpit. "Hey, Rudy. How's it going over there?"

"Roomy and comfortable," Rudy replied. "You?"

"I hate you right now."

Rudy laughed. "I bet. Don't worry, whatever this is won't take long to wrap up. If it's not another attack, we'll be done by dinner."

"Your confidence is...unseemly." Meagan checked her chronometer. "We've got to be getting close."

"If they deploy my guys, they won't want to be *too* close. Hell, I'm thinking they should've sent us ahead."

"Whatever we're after is moving at half the speed of light," Meagan replied. "There's nothing we can do if they don't slow the damn thing down."

"God, if we're leaving that up to the shipboard jockeys…" Rudy clicked his tongue.

"What?" Meagan prompted.

"Oh, we just won't be done until dessert."

Meagan rolled her eyes. "Funny. Let's tap into the bridge coms and listen in. We might get a little warning before having to launch."

"Fine by me."

Meagan initiated the connection and leaned her head back, staring out the top of her cockpit. Voices filled her helmet, people on the bridge going about their duties and talking it through in dry, concise detail. Five seconds of listening in on their jobs made her all the more thankful for her own. Even while sitting in the uncomfortable ship for several hours.

"The vessel is approaching, Commander," Lieutenant Darnell spoke, his voice sounding extra thin over her helmet speakers. "Less than ten minutes to rendezvous."

"I'm picking up a signal," Ensign White said, the communications officer. "Some kind of…repeated message."

"Can you decipher it?" Commander Everly asked. Meagan didn't know what to think of him. On one hand, he seemed like a warmongering ass but he'd always been fair to the men. He may've liked the thrill of battle, the excitement of firing big guns and for that, she couldn't fault him. Part of why she flew involved the adrenaline rush.

"Working on it," Ensign White replied. "It's…strange. Like nothing I've seen before."

"The vessel seems to be reducing speed," Darnell said. "One quarter light speed…a tenth…they've slowed to a crawl."

"Navigation, confirm," Everly said.

"Confirmed, sir." Lieutenant JG Tim Collins piped in. Meagan had no idea how young he was but he must've been only a year out of the academy. She only ran into him once. He got lost in the lower decks and found himself in the pilot's mess. No one looked more out of place. His bookishness and frailty set him apart from the lean, fit fighter jockeys.

"Move to intercept, Redding," Everly said, "but keep our distance."

"Aye, sir. Adjusting position."

"See if we can't get a parallel course," Captain Atwell finally spoke up. Now he was a man Meagan respected. He'd been through some serious shit and maintained a calm, even disposition, the type which made him an amiable leader. She'd served on one of his watches before and he'd been nothing short of a great guy. One of the few COs Meagan harbored no complaints about. "Can you get better scans now, Olly? Maybe help Ensign White?"

"Affirmative, sir." Darnell replied. "The shield's density I talked about before is just an anomaly of design. Now that we're closer, our instruments are no longer blocked. Initiating a sweep."

"Hey, Meagan," Rudy piped in. "I tapped into visual. Sending them over now. This thing…Jesus, it looks like some kind of…I don't know…dinnerware."

"Wow, you're not supposed to tap signals, man." Meagan tapped her knee. "But patch it over to me."

"Yeah, I thought you'd say that. Here you go."

Meagan squinted as her display lit up. The unknown vessel filled her screen, shiny metal shaped like a teardrop. The sharp end led the way and the turbines in the back looked capable of housing a dozen fighters comfortably. A liquid green light surrounded the hull, their version of an environmental shield.

"What the hell…" Meagan muttered.

"I know, right? It looks like they were concerned with aerodynamics or something."

"Or that nose is a weapon," Meagan replied. "God knows it could be. Imagine ramming speed."

"I'd rather not." Rudy gasped. "Hey, did you see that?"

Meagan scrutinized her screen. At first, she had no idea what he was talking about but then, she saw it. A massive panel on the side of the ship opened up, marring the perfect, smooth surface. Olly's voice interrupted her before she could say anything. Apparently, they saw it too and probably had a much better idea of what it meant.

"Report." Commander Everly spoke up. "What is that?"

"Something's coming out of it," Redding said. "Olly, what're you reading?"

"Um…unmanned drones it looks like…a dozen of them…maybe more. Wait, getting an accurate count…twenty-four, all roughly half the size of our Wasp fighters." Olly hummed.

"Group Commander Revente, this is Commander Everly. Launch your fighters but tell them to stay close to the ship. No engagement without word from us, understood?"

Revente replied, "understood, Commander. Launching fighters." A moment later, their own speakers lit up. "Listen up, all fighters prepare for immediate launch. Rules of Engagement are escort only. Do *not* fire unless you receive a direct order from command. Repeat, you will not fire without an order. Fire them up, ladies and gentlemen. This very well might get interesting."

"Here we go Rudy." Meagan shifted her ship from idle to fire up. The pulse drive would reach maximum efficiency in less than twenty seconds. The bombers might take another ten or so but they'd all be out there soon enough. "You sure you're ready?"

"I'm not the girl here, Meagan," he teased.

"How was I confused all this time?" Meagan gripped the flight stick and flexed her fingers.

Unmanned drones. She hadn't fought any of those since the academy. They were wily, able to pull off maneuvers no human pilot could but what they won in squirrelly moves, they lost out on intuition. Human creativity proved victorious over AI controlled crafts seven out of ten times.

Attempts to program them to feel otherwise made too many people nervous. God knows what the AI would do next so they left them dumb. But these weren't constructed on Earth. They were alien and therefore, might be very different. Depending on their proclivity for victory, if this broke into a fight, it could be a real slug fest.

The burners in her ship made the entire frame rumble. The noise in the hangar hammered at her from all sides, making her head numb. When she reached the cold vacuum of space, all that noise would wash away. One of the only things to bother her came from the silence of the void where only the machines in her ship and the voices of command and fellow pilots were audible.

"Panther one, you are cleared for launch," the radio tower operator spoke with his calm aplomb. No matter how wild a situation became, those guys always seemed to play it cool. She wondered if they enjoyed some kind of psychological conditioning or if they took some kind of drug. "Godspeed."

"Thanks, tower." Meagan patched into her squadron. "Panther wing, get ready to fall out. Follow my lead and stay close to the ship. This is strictly escort so lets not screw this up. Anyone have any questions, you can ask in the air but don't fire. Our orders are to keep the ship safe and I suppose we'll know when we're needed. Until then, let's get this party started. I'll see you out there."

Chapter 5

"Readings, Darnell," Adam leaned forward as he spoke. "What're you picking up?"

"It wouldn't have mattered if I gathered data on the hull before, sir." Darnell's fingers flashed over his console, moving with magician like dexterity. "The chemical composition is unknown to all our databases."

"I'm getting sick of hearing that." Adam turned to Clea. "Any clue why our information seems woefully inaccurate?"

Clea shrugged. "Perhaps it's merely brand new, Commander. We didn't chart every single item in the universe, much as we tried."

"What about the drones, Olly?" Gray asked. "Are they armed?"

"Yes, sir. They definitely have weapons. They seem to be similar to our own as do their shields. Defensive barriers are generated from the power core located at the center of each. Since people don't crawl inside, they can be smaller and pack the same punch."

"Brilliant." Everly frowned in thought. "But there's no indication of a power up from the larger ship?"

"If anything, it seems to be powering down. The shields are still up but the engines are off, not even idling. It's very strange." Darnell looked over a couple of charts before speaking again. "I'm getting information from the inside. Oxygen, gravity, heat…at least one of their stations is dedicated to life support and while other things are shutting down, that's still going strong."

"So there must be people on board," Gray said. "How're you able to analyze the atmosphere but not pick up life forms?"

"There's still some interference," Olly said, but didn't sound certain. "The ship's definitely set up to support life…maybe they're in a safe room, something lined in a material defying our scans."

"They might be dead," Clea added, "depending on how long they've been making this journey. The ship must've been programmed to stop when another vessel came too close. I suspect the drones are merely a distraction, something to keep enemies from bothering the thing so it can move on its way."

"Why stop?" Adam shrugged. "It can haul ass, so why risk an engagement?"

Clea tilted her head, observing Adam with her odd, silvery eyes. "A universal similarity concerning starship design is what sub light travel does to the engines. If this ship traveled at top speed, it would be unable to make defensive maneuvers. Inertial dampeners are not sophisticated enough to protect the inhabitants of a vessel from dramatic course changes. It could not respond to any threat."

"The program stops and deploys defensive measures. Hence the drones and why we're keeping our distance. Correct, Captain?"

"We have to figure out what the hell's on board somehow." Gray scratched his chin. "What do you think will happen if we approach the ship?"

"Something will be blown up," Clea answered.

"Not as helpful as I'd hoped." Gray stood, paced toward the screen and clasped his hands behind his back. "If we back off, it'll likely fire up its engines again and speed off, huh?"

"Yes," Clea said. "An automated program would analyze the situation, assess the threat, recall the drones and continue its journey."

"Olly, you talked about shield density," Gray said. "Can our weapons penetrate it?"

"Yes, sir. What I referred to was *how* they generated the shield. I made no particular explanation to its defensive capabilities. All I knew then was I couldn't see past it. Now that we're here, it's pretty much a standard environmental barrier. Powerful enough to deflect debris but not designed for combat."

"And they didn't boost the power when they stopped?" Everly shook his head. "Why?"

"Those drones might be nastier than we think," Gray said. "Ensign White, what's going on with the signal you picked up?"

"I've modified Olly's cypher and added an app of my own," White replied. "It seems to be some kind of greeting…possibly a *hello*. I'll know more in a few minutes."

"We may not have a few minutes," Clea muttered.

"What're your thoughts?" Everly asked Gray.

"I think we need to board it." Gray contemplated the screen for another long moment in silence. "But I'm damn curious what this signal is. If they're genuinely aiming for a peaceful communication, then I don't want to engage. Right now, the only way we're getting in there involves taking out the drones."

"Marshall won't like what we've got," Everly said. "He's going to want more."

"C'mon, Agatha," Gray said to Ensign White. "We need that information."

"I'm working on it, sir." White maintained a reserved tone but a hint of nerves colored the tone. "I'm almost there."

"Can you lock weapons on those things, Redding?" Gray asked.

"Negative, sir. They're too small and fast for our systems to grab on to."

"Our ships can take them," Everly added. "Give the word and I'll have them engage."

"Sir, I've decrypted the message." White let out a sigh of relief. "It states *Greetings, we are the Caerna. Our home was attacked and destroyed by a dangerous enemy which may come after you. Our crew is in suspended hibernation and may require medical aid. We come in peace and hope you will grant us aid, the few who remain of our race.*"

Gray took a deep breath and stared at the screen. Everly's enthusiasm for attack lost gravity in light of the message but the drones put them at a stalemate. The Behemoth could not assist these people without a potential engagement. Peripherally, he heard Revente report that all fighters were in escort position.

That's when the drones made a move.

"Sir, the drones seem to be moving in our direction," Olly said. "We've been scanned...and they are closing in."

"Can you tell if they're weapons hot?" Everly asked.

"Affirmative, sir." Olly nodded. "Weapons are powering up."

"Full shields," Gray announced. "Give the order to engage."

"Aye sir." Everly tapped his tablet. "Revente, your people are go. Take out those drones."

"Affirmative." Revente's voice crackled through the speakers. "We're on it. Patching all coms through to your station for situation updates."

Gray turned to Clea. "Here we go."

"This seems odd." Clea leaned back in her seat. "Why send a peaceful message then attack? I hope this allows us to gather answers without pushing our hand for an ultimate solution. I'd hate to lose any data their computers may hold concerning the enemy. However, if it starts firing..."

"Yes, I know. We might have to take them down." Gray scowled at the view port. "Let's hope it doesn't come to that but if it does, I'll pull the trigger."

Clea nodded. "Of course."

Gray turned to Adam. "Let me know when our fighters are combat operational and get me a tactical display. Let's see if our training paid off, people."

***

"Panther One, this is Giant control."

Here it comes, Meagan thought. She saw the drones moving away from their ship, heading toward the Behemoth and figured they'd be ordered to engage. The last member of her wing barely deployed before the message came.

"You are weapons free. Engage at will and do *not* allow those drones to get within firing range of the Behemoth. Confirm."

"Confirmed, Giant control." Meagan brought the others of her wing up on coms. "Okay, everyone. We've got the green light. Form up and spread out. Don't give them a cluster to fire into and remember your simulations against AI opponents. Should come in handy against these things."

A series of affirmation came from her wing and she grinned inwardly. She'd been working with these folks for over a year, knew them all down to their families, hopes and dreams. Each of them proved to be exceptional pilots and Earth command training made them better. She gladly put her life in their hands and as a result, she endeavored to be the first to deploy, the last to return.

"Squadron Leader Tauran here, Ma'am." Meagan's second, Mick Tauran, proved to be a solid leader but she knew what he had to say. They deployed seven Wasps and Rudy's bomber wing. Twenty-four drones sounded like a tough enemy to brawl. "Are we launching additional fighters?"

"Giant control, this is Panther One," Meagan adjusted her course and the rest of her wing followed suit. They started toward the drones, a trip that would take a good five minutes before they'd meet up. "Are we expecting some backup?"

"Be advised," Giant control replied, "Three more wings will be deployed momentarily. ETA to your position, three minutes."

"There you go, Panther Two," Meagan said. "We'll have plenty of help before the shooting starts. Everyone fire up the weapons and the second you have range, you take a shot. I don't want anyone getting bright ideas of closing distance. Use your superior range to our advantage and don't forget, these machines don't care if they get hit. You do. No unnecessary risks."

Scans showed the launches behind her as the Behemoth let fly additional fighters. Hers was the point of the spear and the others would work to flank the enemy, crushing them in the center of an open space kill box. Whether the larger ship would intervene or not, she refused to guess but a bigger concern came from whether there were more drones or not.

The last thing she wanted was to enter a brawl with over a hundred of those things.

Giant control sent out what data they had to the pilots just after they cleared the hangar. They were predictably maneuverable with equivalent weapons but smaller. They'd be a pain to target but her folks practiced this exact scenario. No combat situation felt sure but this one seemed as close to it as humanly possible.

"Panther One, be advised." Estaban's voice sounded alien when he got all professional. It drove her nuts but they had to follow protocol. "You are twenty-seconds from maximum missile range."

"Giant control, acknowledged. Our scans show us the same thing. Shields are maxed. Here we go."

Fighter violence tended to be carefully controlled chaos. Movement, firing, and maintaining any sense of discipline had to come as second nature or rate of survival dropped by sixty percent. Whatever statistician came up with *that* number probably needed a dose of humanity but she couldn't argue.

"Locking missiles," Panther Four spoke up, Leslie Eddings. She always took the lead in simulations.

Fantastic pilot, definitely a future leader. The others followed suit, rattling off a chorus of attack plans.

"Panther One, on your mark," Mick said. "We're ready."

"Fire and engage. Stick to your wingman and cover each other." A barrage of missiles detached from their vessels, hurtling toward the drones at blinding speed. None of them waited for explosions or contacts. They veered away, two at a time, to gain an advantage in the engagement.

Life became instinct and feedback to Giant control came as second nature. Meagan barely noticed she spoke as she slammed the throttle forward and pulled her ship into a climb. Panther Two stayed close by on the starboard side, meeting her maneuvers as if they were possessed of a symbiotic link. Scans gave her a countdown for when to adjust course for an attack vector, a chance to take a shot at the first of the drones.

"Panther Wing, be advised," Giant control announced. "Initial volley of missiles proved effective against their shields. Splash one through five."

Meagan felt a wave of relief. They had no idea if their weapons would even work on the enemy. Now that they proved to be just like them, wonder left the floor. Now they just had to engage in a by the numbers dogfight, something they'd all encountered more than once in their careers.

Two green blasts sizzled by her cockpit, attacks which barely missed. She jammed her controls to the right and spun, bringing her front end in line with two of the drones. "No time for lock," she muttered, eyeballing her reticle and pulling the trigger for the pulse cannons. Purple-white beams leaped from the cannons near the nose, tearing through space and terminating in a ball of white light.

"Splash six," Meagan announced. The cockpit heated up and she knew it'd get hotter. Every use of her pulse weapons cooked the ship a little and though the sinks would keep her from boiling, comfort was a tertiary concern. Effectiveness mattered a lot more.

"They're all over me!" The announcement made Meagan glance to the left just as three of the drones converged on Panther Eight, Kelly Parson. One of the newest members of her unit, the young lady could handle herself and she spun and dove to get away. The AI kept up, throwing shot after shot at her but so far, intuitive flying kept her alive.

"Panther Seven, where the hell are you?" Meagan diverted her course and headed in to aid the other pilot. "Panther Two, form up and watch my six."

"Affirmative," Mick Replied.

"This is Panther Seven, I've been hit!" Richard Martin, Kelly's wingman, shouted into the com. "I've got operational control but my weapons are offline!"

"Disengage, Panther Seven," Meagan dodged to the right as one of the drones nearly collided with her. Another danger of AI came from their lack of concern for kamikaze tactics, especially if a foe proved to be capable of out flying them. "Panther Eight, hold on. We're almost there."

The other wings from the Behemoth were just engaging but Panther was hip deep in the battle. Drones whizzed by as little more than green blurs, their shields leaving tracers in their wake. The AI didn't appear to employ any guided weapons systems so they didn't have to deal with missiles but the design made them tiny projectiles without it.

"Has anyone been able to get a lock?" Panther Three shouted. "I'm having to guess every shot!"

"Negative," Panther Four replied. "Computers can't keep up."

Jesus, we barely can. Meagan thought, spinning her ship to avoid a collision and entering a heavy dive. It took her out of the mix bowl of violence just long enough to recover, slam the controls to the right and accelerate back into the fight. The magnets whined as they battled inertial and her bones strained from the tension.

A drone moved in behind her and a red light flashed on her scans. *They have a lock, huh? Okay then, let's try this*.

She tilted her stick to the right, allowing the incoming attack to blast over and under her ship. *Let's play follow the leader, you prick.* It would be a dangerous game but one she hoped to use to her advantage.

"Um, Panther One, you are being seriously groped by that drone," Panther Two said. "I'm moving to engage."

"I've got this, Mick," Meagan said, but she fell silent as she fell into deep concentration, focusing all her attention on the subtle maneuvers required to avoid being blown to hell. The drone fired three more times before she got it into the position she wanted. As she plunged full speed into a cluster of other drones, she started a mental countdown from five.

Five…

Another two blasts singed her paint, glancing off the shields. *I don't have too many of those. Pulse blasts will wear down shields. The only thing more effective are missiles*.

Four…

This time, she took a direct hit but the shields held. Her HUD expressed the danger of another hit and advised against it in the same cold, calculated manner that their enemies conducted themselves in the fight. *I'm almost there, c'mon girl. You've got this*.

Three...

Meagan took her fighter down, avoiding another blast, before climbing back to her original heading. The other drones were less than two hundred kilometers away, a heart beat in space combat.

Two...

The drone drew closer and she fought hard to keep her reserve. This would only work if she had nerves of steel, the kind that allowed her to face down three more drones which got wind of her and started a collision course. *Okay, this might've been the stupidest idea you've had in a few lifetimes*.

"One!" Meagan shouted the word and climbed, jamming on the brakes. The drone chasing her fired and dusted one of his own. The other two couldn't slow down. A collision jarred her vessel and Meagan spun the ship so her front faced the carnage. The last of her attackers seemed to be damaged and she used maneuvering thrusters to get a bead...pulled the trigger...

"And that would be three." Meagan announced over the com as another white ball burst and disappeared in the blink of an eye. "How're we doing, Giant control?"

"Be advised, there are six drones left."

Holy crap, we were really on it. Meagan looked around the battlefield and joined back up with Panther Two. Other vessels were tearing it up, veering here and there as they wrapped up engagements with the enemy AI. Debris bounced off their shields, thousands of pieces of computerized space crafts drifted about, becoming a hazard to civilian space travel.

Cleanup crews will be pissed about this one.

"Giant control, this is White Knight One. We have finished the final engagement. No other hostiles on scan."

"Affirmative," Giant control replied. "Good job but stay alert. If anything else comes out of that thing, shoot it down."

"This is our sky now, sir," Meagan replied. "We won't give it up to anyone."

"I'll hold you to that, Meagan. Revente out."

Chapter 6

"The fighters successfully destroyed the drones," Everly announced. "Casualty reports coming in."

"Patch them through to my tablet," Gray said. He sat in his chair and looked over the results. They lost one ship and four more were damaged. Not bad considering the odds but still, worse than he'd hoped for. "Did we recover the pilot from the downed ship?"

"Their ejection pod has been located and we're bringing in their core as well," Everly replied. "They're reporting minimal injuries but we won't know until they hit the sick bay."

"Better than it could've been, worse than I wanted." Gray set the tablet down. "Redding, get us in closer but boost our shields. I don't want any surprises from that thing. If it starts shooting, I want full weapons lock."

"Aye, sir. Maneuvering thrusters activated." Redding paused as she tapped away at her console. "Weapons targeted and locked. Distance?"

"Get us within two hundred kilometers," Olly said. "That should be plenty for me to finally pierce their defenses and finalize our data."

"Okay," Redding engaged the thrusters and the ship started moving. "ETA, five minutes."

"Make sure the fighters clear our path," Gray said.

Everly hit the com control. "Revente, keep your pilots out of our wake."

"Pretty sure they know that without me telling them," Revente replied. "But I'll remind them not to get tossed out into deep space."

Everly shook his head. "He gets a little pissy with the obvious ones."

"Understandable," Clea said. "I've found most humans prefer to be given the benefit of the doubt. Unfortunately, they so rarely deserve it."

"Ouch, Clea." Everly clicked his tongue. "Not exactly a kind observation about my people."

"I'm not trying to be cruel." Clea shrugged. "Let's just say there's a reason soldiers receive orders and people require bosses. Even in my culture, we do have the occasional person who needs corrective action."

"Bring Marshall on the line," Gray said. "Tell him his men better be ready for deployment."

"Marshall, are your boys ready to go?" Everly asked.

"They're in the drop ship but you'd better have more to give me or I'm going to need to draft everyone on board to take that thing."

"We're working on it now," Everly replied. "Relax. We'll feed our scans to your tablet in a few minutes." He muted the com. "I hope you know what you're doing, Olly."

"I do." Olly glanced back and smiled. "I've had plenty of time to study this thing and the drones gave me some insights as well. I'm coding a new algorithm to get through any interference, radiation or otherwise.

This should give me a good indication of what's going on inside and potentially, I'll be able to access any sort of visual equipment they have."

"Won't it be coded in such a way that it won't be compatible with your software?" Clea asked. "Or are you using…" Her eyes widened. "Wait a minute, you're not using our universal translation code, are you?"

Olly's cheeks flushed. "Yes, Ma'am…"

"Where'd you get that?" Clea spun on Gray. "Who granted him access to that data?"

"If I'm not mistaken, Lieutenant Darnell has top clearance for computer based applications." Gray shrugged. "He probably has access to better programs than I do. Hell, he wrote half the ones they're using at the academy now. Why? What's wrong?"

"Someone unfamiliar with our protocols could cause some pretty serious damage with that code, Captain." Clea folded her arms over her chest and glared at him. "I…feel we need to continue this conversation in private."

"And just as soon as we're not in the middle of an operation, I'll listen to your complaint through an entire shift. Right now, I think we should be grateful that Olly took the initiative or we wouldn't get as far as we are with this ship."

Clea shook her head but remained silent, staring out the viewport.

"How long before your new application is ready?" Everly asked.

"A few more minutes...I'll have it in plenty of time to use it when we're in position. Then the marines can do their thing."

"You might need to access hangar control," Gray said. "I don't really want our men having to cut through whatever that is...if we even can."

"Understood. But my scans will show me any weak points in the event we have to breach their hull."

"Sounds good." Gray sat back to wait, one of the hardest things to do as a commander. Everyone around him buzzed through their jobs, coordinating the preparations for a landing, managing the pilots and receiving reports from all over the ship in relation to normal operations. The Behemoth was proving to be a well oiled machine on her first real mission and it filled him with pride...and no small amount of relief.

***

"We're in position," Redding said. "Go ahead, Olly."

"Already on it." Olly put his findings on the view screen for all to see. "It's working! We have access to their information and I have the lifeforms they referred to in their message. There're quite a few."

"Probably not as many as there should be for an entire race," Gray said. "Where are they onboard?"

"They seem to be in the center." Olly tapped at the screen and the view changed, moving the vessel in a circle so they saw it from the top. "Here, roughly dead center."

"Defenses?" Everly asked. "Internal? Automated? Robots?"

"They seem to have automated defenses all attached to three redundant network stations, which are surprisingly not as alien as expected." Olly cleared his throat. "I'll just um…use this code to tap in…"

Clea sighed.

"Sorry, Miss An'Tufal." Olly worked his controls like a pianist playing one of Chopin's etudes. Redding started to say something but he shushed her without looking up, his eyes wide with concentration, face scrunched up in a scowl. An alarm went off, a flashing red light followed by a beeping. "That's okay, don't worry about it, I've got it under control…ish…mostly…"

"Olly…" Everly warned. "What the hell are you doing?"

"The most delicate work of my career, sir." Olly replied. He picked up the pace just when Gray figured there was no way he could move his fingers faster. The alarm abruptly stopped and the light went out. The young technician flopped back in his seat and let out a deep breath, brushing sweat from his brow. "Okay then."

"What did you just do?" Redding demanded. "What was all that?"

"I was hacking into their computer system," Olly said, "when I tripped what would be easiest to describe as their firewall. It...well...it tried to counter hack *our* computer."

"What?" Gray asked. "I don't think I heard you right. We almost got hacked?"

"Sort of. I mean, their AI gave it a college try but I'm...well, I'm pretty good at this."

"You shouldn't have been better than their computer," Clea said. "You took quite a gamble with the universal code. If you'd made a real mistake, that machine could've used the code to easily hack us."

"They didn't," Gray interrupted. "Good work, Olly but next time you decide to endanger everyone on board, do make sure you tell us before hand."

"Aye, sir." Olly swallowed hard.

"So what did your little hack get us?"

"Access to docking procedures. I don't see any databases so those are isolated." Olly paused to read something. "I can get us aboard but in order to gather more data, someone needs to patch in directly."

Gray moved to look over Olly's shoulder. "So you can keep that hangar open?"

"Yes, or rather, I can keep it open." Olly scrutinized the system. "Their guns are offline in there so we won't be attacked right away. Whatever tech we send can access a terminal and use my code to take control of security too...theoretically."

"Send this information to Marshall," Gray said. "Can we get them landed in ten minutes?"

"I'm certain of it." Everly turned to make the arrangements.

Gray considered the screen. "Looks like over one hundred people in there. Do you know what will initiate a wakeup sequence?"

"I'm not sure, sir," Olly said. "Those systems aren't available for remote access. I'd have to be on board to figure it out."

Redding smirked. "You want to go hang out with the marines?"

"Er…not particularly. Not because they aren't cool but just… you know I just…don't like field work much."

"Tough," Everly said. "Once they've secured the area, we'll send you over to take a look. Maybe you can find their databases and we can fill in some of these gaps we've identified today."

"Oh…sounds great, sir." Olly slumped in his seat.

"I'd like to go as well," Clea said. "I need to see these people myself."

Gray nodded. "Sounds good. You'll have operational command over the technical staff. Marshall maintains security."

Clea nodded. "Understood."

"Everly, let's get those marines aboard and take this ship." Gray returned to his seat. "I want the *Silver Star* under our control as soon as possible."

Clea smirked. "Naming the ship now, are we?"

"It seems fitting," Gray replied. "Proceed with the operation, Commander."

***

Marshall Dupont stood in his tactical room with two aides, watching the screen as the drop ship departed for the foreign vessel. He wore a grave expression, hands held tightly behind his back. Sending good men into unknown situations irked him but he agreed they needed to take the ship. With no indication whether they'd encounter opposition, he didn't feel good about putting lives at risk.

Captain William Hoffner commanded the boarding operation. He left with two squads, twenty six men each. His objective was to establish a beach head so the next two squads could board with a technical team in tow. Together, they would take the vessel, access the computer system and gather all available data.

The second wave followed the first, giving them plenty of space to board and report back. Intelligence stated tech crews were unable to access the defensive matrix aboard the vessel so remote hacking wouldn't work. Despite the friendly message from the ship, they'd already proven to be aggressive with their drones.

Were they actually there for a fight, using the message as a ruse? Or did something malfunction? Reports suggested the ship had been in transit for a long time. Damage or merely a lack of maintenance might account for problems. He knew some of the men hoped the drones simply went crazy but he knew better than to rely on wishful thinking.

"This is Captain Hoffner," Will's voice crackled over the speakers. "We are on approach vector. Shields are fully powered and we have not experienced any hostile activity. Next update in one minute."

"Acknowledged." Marshall replied. "Cameras are live. All signals are strong."

The drop ship approached, closing in on the open hangar. A nose sensor provided data back to the command center. Darkness bathed the hangar, making the entrance an oppressive maw. Fortunately, they gathered decent information about the interior and knew enough to make a tactical landing.

Life support functioned inside, meaning it would support life but regardless, Marshall had his men in armored environmental suits. If the drones did malfunction, anything could. The last thing he wanted was a death due to something as mundane as a lack of oxygen or a sudden burst of radiation from open space.

At least Atwell and the bridge crew let him do his job without meddling. One of the best parts of serving aboard the Behemoth was the autonomy to handle missions however he saw fit. Their contribution tended to be limited to stating an objective and trusting he'd get them done. He made a deal before he came on board related to the situation.

He wouldn't tell them how to conduct a naval battle, they wouldn't bust his chops over ground ops.

"Entering the ship," Will announced. "Kicking on the lights."

Marshall watched as the hangar illuminated, revealing smooth walls and neatly ordered mechanical devices standing from floor to ceiling. At first guess, he figured they must be used to repair the drones if they return from a mission but they didn't look like anything on Earth with their thin arms and dozens of tendrils hanging from silver box frames.

I hope those aren't sentries. God knows we don't need to deal with octopod robots.

"Analyzing the area," Will said. "Life support levels are stable. All equipment in the hangar is powered off. We are landing the craft and preparing to disembark. Beach head should be established in less than five minutes."

"Take it by the numbers, Captain," Marshall said. "Don't do anything crazy."

"Wouldn't dream of it, sir. Right now, we're seeing nothing at all. I wouldn't exactly call this a hot LZ. When we have the hangar, we'll clear the door and invite the other ship to come in for a landing."

So far so good.

"Let's get it done." Marshall didn't let himself relax, much as he thought he probably could. Anything might still happen. Until they had the data and got off that invading tub, he wouldn't feel comfortable. At least his men seemed calm. Whether they maintained their confidence through ignorance of the situation or belief in their abilities, he couldn't say.

Regardless, he felt like the right people were on the job. Now to finish it up.

Chapter 7

And this is why I hate field work. Olly sat amidst a bunch of marines, all armed and armored for an epic battle. They stuffed him in his suit as well but instead of a massive rifle, he carried a combat hardened tablet and a sidearm. *Are these guys genetically modified? How the hell are they so big?*

Ground forces definitely recruited from a place where they grew them big. Olly stood at five-eight and the shortest man who boarded the drop ship with him stood six-one. The armor added bulk to their shoulders, granting them a monstrous visage. Intimidation value went a long way in combat and these men had that in abundance.

"Hey, geek," the guy sitting to his right nudged him. "Can you patch us in to the landing crew on your tablet?"

"Um…yeah but it's not exactly protocol to tap lines…"

"You serious?" Another marine said. "Don't be like that. Just patch us in. We want to know what we're dealing with down there."

"Yeah, okay…" Olly took a deep breath and tapped away at the screen. A moment later, they saw a number of small images, each depicting the camera of one of the soldiers already aboard the ship. "There we go."

"They're a little small…hey! Click on Johnson."

"Yeah," the next marine said. "If anything goes down, he'll be in front of it."

"Sure…uh…this one?" Olly tapped an image.

"Yep, that's the one." They laughed together and the first one spoke again, "looks pretty boring. This is a milk run, man."

"God damn it." His companion shook his head. "They didn't need all of us for that."

"What if it turns out to be something else?" Olly offered. The looks they gave him made him speak quickly. "I mean, you know…it could be pretty crazy down there…we won't know for a bit…right?"

"You'd better hope for your sake it isn't crazy. You ain't exactly equipped for violence."

Olly refused to argue. He didn't want to be there and knew his sole contribution involved working with the tech crew. Despite being given command over four other people, he didn't feel any excitement. A wild night for him involved journals and studying. Flying into a potential combat zone vastly exceeded the limits of his nerves.

"This is Captain Hoffner," the voice piped through the speakers. "The LZ is clear and you're authorized to land."

"Here we go, geek." Olly's marine partner nudged him again. "Won't be exciting but at least you're off the bridge."

"Yeah, that's *exactly* what I wanted." Olly sighed.

"Just stay in the back with the others. You'll be fine." The ship set down gently off to the side of the other. When the door dropped, the marines fell out like they were taking a beach head, leaving Olly and the four technicians behind. They exchanged confused glances before heading out at a normal pace.

Olly's team consisted of some of the newest techs onboard, Ensign Maria Anderson, Ensign Gregory Trudeau, Lieutenant JG Lisa Oxton and Ensign Cathleen Brooks. Their aptitude tests were off the charts and they earned their place on the Behemoth. Olly put a lot of faith in their abilities, even if their task involved the most *unknown* tech of his career.

Captain Hoffner approached and motioned away from the entrance. "The door's over there. We found a computer panel of some kind. See what you can do."

"Yes, sir." Olly motioned with his head for his companions to follow.

Behind them, a shimmering green light protected them from the hazards of space, the environmental shield holding back the vacuum. They had to be careful about what they tampered with. Even though they wore environmental suits with magnetic boots, there were other dangers from space beside radiation and a lack of air.

Debris striking the ship would definitely make their trip quick.

Two marines guarded the door, flanking it on either side. One moved for Olly and his companions to gain access to the console Hoffner spoke of. It was little more than a flat black display with no access ports or holes of any kind. *This is going to take some dismantling. It has to be connected somehow...and maybe we can access it that way.*

"Lisa, what's your opinion?" Olly asked. He'd taken a military command class at the academy. The instructor said one of the best ways to build and maintain morale involved including your subordinates in problem solving. They all have skills and talents, he lectured. Let them show you.

"We'll probably need to cut through the wall to gain access to their network," Lisa said. "I recommend a full scan of the wall here so we don't screw up and cut through a conduit we need."

"Alright, you're on scans." Olly turned to Gregory. "I'd like you to take a stroll and look over those devices, see what you can pick up with your tablet. I want to know if they're receiving power and could come back on and if we should be worried about it."

"Got it, sir."

"The rest of you hang back." Olly turned his attention to Lisa's activities. "I have a feeling we'll all have plenty to do in a few minutes."

Lisa pressed her tablet against the wall but withdrew when the black panel brightened and a squiggly line rushed across from left to right. "Greetings," an overhead speaker belted the voice. Marines aimed their weapons. Olly rolled his eyes. "Welcome, human beings. I am the Synthetic Intelligence Device for this vessel. Thank you for answering our distress call."

"How the hell does it speak English?" A marine asked, nudging Olly.

The computer responded, "I've been scanning your vessel and listening to your speech. It did not take long to assimilate and find a method to easily communicate with you. Please let me know if you wish to speak in a different tongue. I have also learned your Russian."

"English will be fine," Olly said. "So…Synthetic Intelligence Device…are you an AI?"

"That is correct, sir. I am a highly advanced artificial intelligence capable of over two hundred thousand commands and functions."

"Mind if we call you Sid? It's just a little shorter than…" Olly shrugged. "What you said you are."

"You may refer to me in whatever manner best suits your needs. I will respond to Sid."

"Perfect! Um…we understand your crew is in suspended animation. We'd like to wake them up."

"Many of our systems are offline, including some of the automated repairs. I would be happy to walk your technicians through the necessary repairs if you would be so inclined to assist."

"We would." Olly nodded, then scolded himself for the unnecessary gesture. "What about your database? We'd like to see what happened to your people."

"All storage banks are currently offline. Restoration will require manual intervention."

"Okay, can you close the hangar door and open this to the hallway?" Olly asked. He looked back at the marines and had an idea. "Also, are there any automated defenses we have to worry about? Any guns you might want to shut down for us?"

"Negative, our internal security is offline. Restoration will require manual intervention."

"Good. Let's get these doors taken care of and we'll get started." Olly looked back at the marines and other technicians. "Sound good to you?"

Hoffner scowled. "We'll still be clearing corridors before rushing along. First squad, two by two, men. Cover your partners and stay alert. I don't want any surprises as we get deeper into this ship. I'll stay with second squad and maintain security. I want our ass to be protected."

A whole lot of loud acknowledgement went on and Olly turned to his people. "Gregory, stick around and finish the survey on this gear. It might come in handy, especially if it's maintenance related. The rest of you should come with me. I suspect I'm going to need you all in order to bring this place back online."

People got into position, preparing to head out of buckle down.

"Sid, I suspect we'll need parts to restore services," Olly said." Is there a storage area with such equipment?"

"Of course. When you have examined the damage, I will direct you to the location of our stores. I think you will find we are adequately stocked for all your maintenance needs."

"That's reassuring," Lisa muttered. "Will you be able to communicate with us all throughout the ship?"

"My systems still function enough for communication in every department aboard, yes."

The hangar door closed behind them. Hoffner's com went crazy and Olly knew that it must be Lieutenant Colonel Dupont asking what the hell happened. He watched the marine commander step away to answer some questions just as the hallway door opened.

Everyone waited for the quick briefing to end before the soldiers started clearing the path.

The hallway was smooth, silvery metal with no open access chutes or exposed pipes and wiring. They could see their reflections in the walls, floor and arched ceiling and it felt like a funhouse from a crazy carnival. A blue light appeared above them, glowing seemingly beneath the surface. It led off in one direction, heading down a twisting hallway which made it impossible to see to the end.

"Sid," Olly said, "can you define the chemical compound of the ship surface? Is it the same as the hull?"

"Affirmative," Sid replied. "I'm sending it now."

Olly looked over his tablet and his eyes widened.

"What is it?" Lisa nudged him.

"The closest thing I can approximate it to is a diamond…but they inject impurities to strengthen it, much like we do with carbon on steel alloy." Olly shook his head. "Both internal and external are the same. It's like the ship was made out of one large piece of this substance. Cutting it would've been…well, it would've required a pulse blast I think."

"Amazing…" Maria turned and observed the wall. "And it's so smooth. They must've had specialized equipment to make these tunnels."

"That explains why the roof is beveled," Cathleen added. "Maybe they just went through here with a boring device or vehicle."

"It feels pretty alien," Olly replied. "We're used to flat ceilings when they're this low. The closest naturally occurring thing I can think of is like an insect hive."

"Do you think bugs built this ship?" One of the marines threw that out.

"Doubtful," Olly said, "but possible, sure. I mean, what isn't possible?"

"Follow the blue line on the ceiling to the suspended animation chamber," Sid announced. "There, you can address many of the problems aboard. Things will have to be handled in stages, I'm afraid. In order to keep those who are sleeping alive."

"We'll map out the steps when we get there," Olly said. "How long have you been traveling?"

"Time has a different meaning for the people who built this vessel but studying yours, the equivalent is one year, three months, seventeen days, six hours and nineteen minutes."

"Very precise measurement." Olly looked back at Lisa, pausing as the Marines cleared the next hallway. He addressed Sid again, "why did you leave?"

"That information is currently locked. I cannot access it at this time."

"Did something happen to your planet?"

"That information is currently locked. I cannot access it at this time."

Lisa spoke up. "Can you define the current boundaries of your database access?"

"Normally, I am able to utilize all the information stored aboard this vessel. However, due to damage, I am cut off."

"Is that why the drones became aggressive?" Olly asked.

"The drone program is designed for defensive measures. When your small ships took position around the larger, their If/Then statement suggested hostile activity. They moved in for violence and I could not stop them. They were entirely automated on a separate subsystem which has been severed from my control."

"Makes sense," Maria said. "But what caused all this damage? We didn't fire on you."

"That information is currently locked. I cannot access it at this time."

"So pretty much anything involving this ship leaving its system and how it got here is off limits," Cathleen said. "I guess we should just be happy it can talk to us about anything at all."

They spent the next hour moving through the ship slowly, allowing the marines to ensure safe passage along the way. Lisa and Cathleen had their scanners going constantly, waving them around to gather readings about the ship. Olly refrained from doing the same. He contemplated their situation, trying to anticipate what exactly they'd be expected to do.

"You are arriving at your destination," Sid announced. "I am opening the door."

The marines stood back, aiming their weapons at a wall which seemed to melt away. Beyond, a number of long cylinders lined the walls, each hooked up to a glowing globe roughly the size of a beach ball. Each was covered in the same silvery metal that made up the ship, with no view port to see inside.

"Whoa…" Olly paced in a circle, taking it all in. "This is…simply incredible."

"You have arrived at the destination. If you will approach the flashing console, we can begin prioritizing the repairs."

"There must be hundreds of them," one of the marines said. "Jesus Christ, is this their whole race?"

"I hope not," Lisa said. "Or they qualify for being extremely endangered."

Olly headed over to the computer. "Lisa, Cathleen, grab some readings off those…globe things. Maria, you're with me."

They spread out and approached the flashing console, which was little more than a bump in the wall with another black screen breaking up the silver. When Olly stood in front of it, the squiggly lines representing Sid appeared. "Simply tap the screen and we can begin."

Olly reached out a tentative hand, exchanging glances with Maria before touching it. A series of characters displayed, building a list of some sort. Half a second later, red lights flashed overhead and Sid shouted 'Alert! Alert!'

"What the hell did you do?" One of the marines asked Olly.

"Nothing! I just touched the screen! It was working then…this!"

"Well what's happening?"

Maria checked her tablet. "It's responding to something it found on a long range scan."

Olly looked over her shoulder. "Oh no…"

"What is it?" The marine asked. "What do you see?"

"Alert," Sid said. "Hostile vessels incoming. Hostile vessels incoming. Initiate Protocol Seven immediately."

"What is protocol seven?" Olly asked.

"The chance these people lost their homes to protect. A weapon against the enemy."

"Excellent! How do we initiate protocol seven?"

"That information is currently locked. I cannot access it at this time."

"God damn it!" Olly sighed and paced away. "Can we get access if we fix this stuff?"

"Affirmative." Sid sounded all too cheery. "Prioritization almost complete."

"Establish a channel with the Behemoth bridge," Olly said. "Get me Commander Everly right away. They're back...and what might be our one chance to stop them is hidden in a databank on this ship."

"What's that mean?" Maria asked.

"It means we might be the only thing that can save Earth from another attack," Olly said. "Providing the Behemoth can beat them back long enough for us to do it."

"Line established," Cathleen said, handing him her tablet. "Direct com to the bridge."

"Commander, Captain, this is Lieutenant Darnell. As I'm sure you've seen from our early warning, we have another set of visitors but this time, I don't think they plan to be as nice. This time, I think we'll have a fight on our hands and I've got a good news/bad news situation here. I hope you're ready for it."

Cause I sure as hell am not, but here we go.

Act 2

Chapter 8

"Commander," Agatha summoned Everly. "I've got Olly on the com."

"I think I know what he's calling about," Ensign Paul Bailey sat at Olly's post, filling in while the Lieutenant was gone. "I'm picking something up on the early warning system. Two large objects, moving fast. They seem to be ships…just shy the size of the Behemoth."

Clea turned to Gray, brows raised. "The plot thickens."

"Put Olly on," Everly said.

"Patched in, sir," Agatha replied.

"Go ahead, Olly. What's going on?"

"I'll make it really quick, sir." Olly took a deep breath and went. "We're aboard the ship and proven that they are friendly but the vessel has experienced some pretty major damage to internal systems. We're working on getting these back online but it's going to take some time. Sid is helping to the best of its ability but it can't access everything we need until we perform progressive repairs."

"Who is Sid?" Everly jumped in.

"The Artificial Intelligence, sir," Olly replied. "It's…well, a long story."

"One we don't have time for." Gray added. "Is that all you've got?"

"No, sir. This ship as well as my tablet picked up the intruders coming in hot. I assume Paul's got them up already?"

"I do, Olly," Paul called out. "They're really hauling."

Everly cleared his throat and asked, "do you know who they are already?"

"This ship identified them as the enemy."

Clea watched as the humans in the room stiffened. Even knowing the possibility didn't prepare them for the news. Their mettle was about to be tested and whether or not this civilization survived rested entirely on their shoulders. How many of them knew that, she didn't know but even if they didn't have that specific information, the gravity of an attack was plenty to garner serious attention.

"How does it know?" Gray asked.

"Apparently, they already wiped out their home," Olly explained. "But there's a silver lining...of sorts."

"Don't mince words." Gray leaned forward. "Just tell us what you've got."

"Something called *Protocol Seven*. Sid called it a weapon against the enemy but..."

"Go on," Everly prompted.

"When I asked it to initiate this weapon, it said it couldn't access it without repairs."

Redding sighed.

"What's it going to take to get that thing operational?" Everly tapped his arm rest. "How long will you need?"

"I can't say yet, sir. We were just cataloging the damage when the alert went off and those ships arrived."

"We'll buy you the time you need," Gray said. "You'll have to get propulsion online though. I can't promise we can stay in this one spot."

"Hold on, let me find out. It moved here so I'm pretty sure we can just fire up the engines again." Olly put them on mute for a moment.

Clea turned to the others. "You know their typical tactic. Like the Blitzkrieg from your World War Two. They're going to come in fast and hard."

"I know." Gray nodded. He stood and put a hand on Reddings chair. "Stephanie, I need you to initiate thrusters and start us drifting to the side. Full weapons ready to fire on my command."

"Without a lock, sir?"

"A lock will tip our hand. Eye ball it. A full spread can do some damage or at least, slow their forward momentum. Then, we'll really let them have it."

"Aye, sir." Redding tapped away at the console and began to move the ship.

"Paul, full scan on those ships," Gray said. "I need to know what their shields are like. Everly, have the fighters ready to do harassment maneuvers. Bombers should prepare for a full pulse run on those things."

Everly got on the com. "Revente, get your fighters into position for attack. Bomber squadrons on standby for orders."

"They're running combat shields, sir," Paul said. "Far more dense than the...the Silver Star."

"Alright, good to know." Gray turned to Clea. "Check my facts. We have to weaken the shields for pulse bombs to cause any real damage, correct?"

Clea nodded. "Yes, but powerful as pulse bombs are, they may not be able to destroy their vessels even with weakened shields. We can, as you've said before, give them a bloody nose, however."

"Might be all we need to accomplish to give Olly the time he needs." Gray sat back down. "Agatha, send a message to Earth Defense and brief them on the situation. Hostile craft incoming and we are engaging. Inform them of our progress with the Silver Star and what we're planning."

"I'm on it, sir," Agatha replied.

Everly turned to Gray. "The fighters are in position. Bombers are standing by."

"I need an ETA." Gray looked at Paul. "Can you give us a count down?"

"Less than ten minutes."

"What the hell?" Everly shook his head. "How'd they get here so fast?"

"I'm reading signs of a hyperjump," Paul explained. "Any closer and we would've been caught up in it."

"Shall we raise the shields?" Everly asked Gray.

"Not yet. Get them ready. I want to lure them in."

"They won't fire until they are close enough to destroy us with a single shot," Clea explained. "This makes the Captain's plan a distinct possibility. We may well be able to take them out if we're lucky."

"What a victory that would be," Gray said, "but I'm not holding my breath."

"Seven minutes," Paul said."

"Are they picking up speed?" Everly sounded incredulous.

Paul nodded. "Aye, sir. Their weapons are powering up."

"Are we in position yet?" Gray asked Redding.

"Thirty seconds at current speed. Shall I increase?"

"Enough to get us there in ten seconds." Gray leaned forward, squinting at the view screen. "Get your finger on the trigger."

"I'm ready to fire on your mark, sir." Redding took a deep breath and scrutinized her screens. She made several adjustments, nodding when she seemed satisfied with what she saw. "Aim adjusted. We should be clear for a good shot."

"Targets are now within maximum range," Paul said. "Closing fast."

"Give them another few moments."

"Whites of their eyes?" Clea said.

Gray smirked. "Something like that."

They could easily see the vessels now, their shields glowing as they plunged through space at a wildly high velocity. According to the report, they would pass over the Behemoth rather than ram into them. This remained consistent with the first attack. Their weapons seemed to be on the bottoms of their ships. Gray hummed softly as a thought occurred to him.

"Redding, roll us five degrees, port side moving up. I want to tear at their bellies."

"Aye, sir but I'll have to recalculate for my aim."

"Shouldn't be too off. Make it happen."

The ship rumbled for a brief moment as the thrusters engaged, rolling the ship as Gray instructed."

"They'll be on us in less than two minutes," Paul said. "They are weapons hot and…yes, I'm reading a surge of power. They're about to fire."

Gray nodded. "Fire at will, Redding."

Space lit up as their weapons blasted away. The enemy ships didn't get their chance to fire before the pulse shots hammered at their shields. Even without lock, many of the weapons connected with their targets. Redding's aim turned out to be far better than Clea would've given her credit for.

Light compensators kicked in, dimming the view screen as blasts flashed against the enemies shields. In the soundless void of space, a litany of chaos raged in silence. The enemy ships attempted evasive maneuvers and threw off their own shots. One cleanly missed and the other grazed the Behemoth's shields, giving it a good shake.

"Glancing hit," Paul announced. "No damage, shields holding."

"And on them?" Gray asked.

"Several direct hits, sir," Paul scanned his console for a quiet moment. "Other ships are showing signs of medium and light damage. Their shields are holding but definitely weakened on the bottoms. They've slowed down as well and their weapons are redirecting."

"Send in the fighters to cover the bombers," Gray said. "Give those bastards some pulse bombs."

"Revente, you're clear to attack," Everly said, the tension in his voice giving it a harsh edge. "Fighters covering bombers. Give them a serious kick in the ass before they can regroup."

Clea leaned toward Gray. "Those fighters better be wily. They're big enough to lock on to."

"They've got good shields," Gray replied. "They can take at least one direct hit."

"I hope you're right."

"They're firing!" Paul shouted. "Incoming!"

"Evasive," Gray said to Redding, too late. The ship rattled as three direct hits splashed against the shields. The motion stopped almost as fast as it began. "Report! Damage?"

"Pulse shields holding," Paul said. "Slight concussion damage on decks seven and eight. No casualties reported as of yet."

"Return fire as the fighters get into position," Gray said. "Full lock and burn."

"Weapons locked and firing," Redding replied, slamming her hand down on the console. Their ship shook again, this time with the force of their cannons firing back at the enemy. Another flash erupted in space as shields and pulse blasts met in a fiery explosion. "Direct hit."

"More medium damage," Paul said. "The fighters have engaged."

"On screen."

Clea stood up and watched as the fighters began harassing maneuvers around the larger vessels. Their smaller weapons caused tiny flashes all over the surface of the enemy shields, like fireworks on the American Fourth of July. Missiles flared and detonated and the bombers lumbered forward, carrying what might be a deadly payload.

"Captain, this is Olly," they heard his voice over the speaker. "Sid has the engines up and running. We can now move."

"Get your ass in gear, Olly," Everly shouted. "Set course for zero-three-alpha seven. Best possible speed. We'll be right behind you."

"Aye, sir."

The Silver Star engines burst to life and the ship pulled away. It turned, heading away from Earth. "Why that direction?" Clea asked. "What're you planning, Commander?"

"To lure the enemy away from Earth," Everly said. "And give us some more room to fight."

More blasts erupted around them, near misses and glances. The ship rattled but held, no real damage occurred. Casualties came in, mostly from being jostled about. Fighters gave the enemy a lot of hell, keeping them mostly busy and unable to direct their focus on the Behemoth.

"Bombers are nearly in range," Paul announced, then gasped. "Shit! One of our fighters is down!"

Everly stood. "Ejection?"

Paul paused. "No…no, sir. I'm afraid not."

"Damn it!"

Gray looked grim. "Casualties, Commander. Their sacrifice won't be in vain. Distance for bombers?"

"They're practically down their throats."

"Have them deploy and issue an RTB for all ships." Gray said. "Once they're clear of our blast, hit them with everything we've got."

"Weapons are locked," Redding said.

"Set a rendezvous course with the Silver Star, Tim." Gray looked at his tablet before continuing, "as soon as the ships are all on board, gun it. I want to put some distance between us immediately. We'll enter a rolling gun battle if we have to."

"Bombers on speaker, Captain." Everly tapped something on his tablet and they heard Rudy Hale speaking to his wing.

"Alright, folks, it's time to see if these things can crack." Rudy lacked any concern at all. No tension, no worry, no stress. He sounded like he carried on a conversation at a party with all the bluster of a man wholly unconcerned. "Fire away!"

To call them bombers was a slight misnomer. The reality involved heavy ordinance, much like bombs of old, but basically guided missiles. These devices, roughly a quarter of the size of a Wasp fighter, moved slowly but caused massive damage. When they fired them at the enemy vessels, sixteen total shots in all, they hoped for the best.

Each weapon came online, showing on the scans as if they were vessels unto themselves. They lumbered toward the enemy vessels, which engaged their engines, pulling away from the battleground. Rudy's ships rushed back toward the Behemoth, clearing a path for the cruiser's weapons to have an open shot.

"Bombs are away," Everly said, "Our fighters are heading for the hangars. It'll be tricky to dock while moving."

"They've trained for it," Gray said, "Open fire, Redding."

Their weapons discharged, joining the bombs as they cut through the dark of space and flared the enemy shields. A few desperate volleys came back their way but the Behemoth's shields held strong. A moment later, the bombs began to detonate, massive balls of white light pummeling the enemy's shields.

"Direct hits all over them!" Paul cried. "Wait...I...I misread that. They've..."

"What?" Everly prompted. "Spit it out!"

"It seems they were able to target the bombs and knock them out before contact. Not with weapons though...some kind of signal caused them to blow early. There was some damage to the shields but nothing like we hoped."

"They're still pulling away," Tim said. "Navigation shows we're gaining distance."

"Regrouping," Clea corrected. "They won't let us get away."

"The fighters have docked," Everly said. "And the bombers are almost all accounted for."

"Give the Silver Star some distance," Gray ordered. "And keep us between them and our guests. When they decide it's time for round two, I want to give them some serious hell."

"They won't fall for those last tactics again, Captain," Clea replied. "They won't charge again."

"Good. That means they'll have to face us toe to toe or not at all. Either way, we've bought the Silver Star some time to get repaired and find us that Protocol Seven."

"As you say, sir." Clea turned to her own tablet. "I'll compile data on the attack and see if I can analyze it for weaknesses, anything to give us an advantage."

"I think we just proved we have it," Everly replied. "This ship's more than they can handle."

"Don't get cocky, Adam." Gray went to Paul's station and peered over his shoulder. "We might be ready for them but that doesn't mean they don't have some serious tricks of their own. This won't be an easy won fight. Let's just keep the distance advantage and get a fresh set of pilots ready. We're going to need them."

Chapter 9

"They're really giving each other hell out there," Lisa shouted from her position near one of the globes, staring at her tablet. A group of marines gathered around her, watching the screen as well. They mumbled quietly together but their excitement filled the room, despite their quiet. "The Behemoth really dished out some firepower."

"What're you doing?" Olly asked from his console. He monitored the engines to ensure they'd stay on, working with Sid to regulate continuous power to propulsion. Maria crouched beside him, running a diagnostic to gather the extent of damage on the ship.

"Watching the battle, sir," Lisa replied. "The Behemoth is following us and the enemy has given them some distance. I think the first engagement's over."

"You're supposed to be gathering data on those globes," Olly said. "Focus, Lieutenant or the next battle you're watching could be our last."

"Can you patch our helm cams in?" One of the marines asked, followed by a litany of nodding. Olly sighed.

"Just make it quick. We have to hurry."

Maria sighed and rubbed her eyes. "Sir, this ship's got serious problems. My diagnostics show we need to reroute power through several conduits."

"We can't replace it?" Olly said.

"It would take a *lot* more time. I'm currently mapping out anything that hasn't completely succumbed to corrosion but if we have to start stringing cables around..."

"We don't have to put them through the walls, do we? Not just to get things working."

"No, if it comes to that, we can string them down the halls...if we have enough length." Maria shrugged. "The corridors here twist and turn. They don't make a lot of sense. More distance will need to be covered by whatever we replace."

"Fair point." Olly frowned at Maria's screen. "You're not kidding."

"I know, right? We've got a lot of work to do."

"Let's get Sid access to this section here," Olly pointed. "That's the centralized computer system. Once it's in, we should be able to gain access to data points pertaining to the Protocol Seven stuff. Plus, I figure it's close by so shouldn't be too bad to fix up."

"I'm on it sir."

Olly's com flashed and he engaged. "Darnell here."

"This is Gregory, sir. I've finished gathering readings from these devices in the hangar. They're essentially automated repair stations. You put in spare parts and it fixes stuff up as you go. Pretty incredible tech, too. My readings suggest they could get one of those drones back to operational status in a quarter of the time a human mechanic would require."

"Amazing. Are they online?"

"Power's cut right now but I see the problem. Do you want me to bring them back online?"

"Get the power routed but don't crank them on," Olly said. "You never know when they might come in handy."

"On it, sir."

"I'm picking up readings in the belly of the ship," Cathleen announced. "Did you guys do anything?"

"Kind of…" Olly replied. "I've been working with Sid on service restoration while Maria maps the conduits." He addressed the console. "What's going on?"

"Power has been routed to the fabrication chamber," Sid replied cheerfully. "I have begun reconstructing the recently lost drones."

Maria looked sharply up. "Is that a good idea? We didn't have control of them before."

"Lieutenant Darnell has restored my services to the security bay. I have ensured the programming recognizes your crew as guests and not invaders. No hostilities toward the Behemoth or her people will be initiated. You are all safe."

"That's a relief," one of the marines muttered.

"What's going on up there?" Captain Hoffner's voice piped through the speakers. "We're hearing a lot of activity somewhere in the ship."

"One second, sir," Olly said. He turned to Sid. "Will it even matter? How long does it take to generate a drone?"

"The fabrication center is quite large and takes up the majority of the center of this craft. I can turn out a functional drone every twenty minutes. It takes another ten to transport them to the various hangars. If we double production, which is quite possible, we can get two point five out every half hour. This puts a strain on the manufacturing facility but can be quite important during combat."

"Will it have any side effects on what we're trying to fix up here?" Maria asked. "We can't afford to lose time on our current work."

"No, ma'am. Now that I'm patched back in, I've set the generators down there to stand alone. They will operate without any impact on other ship systems."

"It's a wonder you guys lost to the enemy," Olly said. He patched through to Captain Hoffner. "Sir, Sid has cranked on a manufacturing plant to build more drones which we should be able to deploy against the enemy and it's doing it pretty fast too. I expect they'll be able to actually provide some assistance, albeit minor, soon."

"Is that safe, Darnell?"

"Yes, sir. I believe so."

"We're going to check it out," Hoffner replied. "I think we'll map out the rest of the ship and see if we can find anything you need. That includes securing the supply bay where the spare parts will be found."

"Fantastic," Olly said. "Please let us know if there's anything we can do to help."

"Likewise, keep us informed of anything else you do. Hoffner out."

"He sounded unhappy," Maria said.

"Don't worry about it," a passing marine said. "He never sounds happy."

"I'll keep that in mind." Maria and Olly exchanged glances. "I'm going to start rerouting now. I've found some decent paths to bypass many of the damaged systems. I'm guessing...fifteen to twenty minutes to pull it off."

"Sounds good...but if you can hurry..."

"Yeah, yeah, I'll do what I can, sir."

"Lieutenant?" Lisa called. "These globes, I've finally got some readings on them."

"Report." Olly couldn't believe he got to use the word. It'd been directed at him so often, he figured he'd never have the chance to toss it at someone else. Now that he did, he couldn't help but smirk.

"These are essentially portable generators to keep the chambers going in the event of power failure. They're remarkable because they recharge fast when not in use and would afford each tube a good eight to thirty hours of power in the event of energy interruption."

Olly raised a brow. "Eight to thirty is a huge difference. Why the discrepancy?"

"The things are playing havoc with my tablet. That's the best I can do before I finish my evaluation."

"Keep it up and let me know. Maybe we can use these to power the whole chamber and wake somebody up."

"Okay, I'll keep working on it."

"Sir, I might have access to a few tables on the database," Cathleen said. "I've just found a backdoor into one of the file servers."

"Really? How?"

"I saw an open connection through this console over here and tried it. Shockingly, it let me in and I'm rebooting this particular segment. I might gain full access."

"Great work!" Olly truly was impressed. "Did you discover anything right away?"

"Just some fringe bits of data. A couple of lines I'm having Sid translate. The first thing to come through states that the people who entered those chambers had no idea what to expect. This part of the technology was brand new to them."

"Wow, they risked a lot," Lisa said. "Crawling into those things without *knowing* they'd wake up again? Scary."

"Seriously." Cathleen shook her head. "I'll let you know when it finishes."

"Sounds good, Olly said. "In the meantime, help Maria get this working. I'm going to keep trying to bring systems online. This ship's a gold mine of power pockets and auxiliary systems. I'm guessing we're standing in a prototype…an untested one."

"That information is currently locked. I cannot access it at this time."

Olly repeated Sid, "I cannot access it at this time, yeah, I know." He tapped away and continued to work. *But that won't be the way it is for long, buddy. Don't worry, I'll get your access back. Sooner or later, you'll remember everything this ship planned to tell the friendly culture that found it and then we'll drive the enemy back.*

Just hold together for me and we've got this.

***

Hoffner lead a small contingency of marines away from the hangar and in the opposite direction the technical crew went. He brought five men, each trailing behind to watch their six as they progressed deeper into the vessel. The long, smooth hallway seemingly went on forever, twisting and turning in seemingly random directions.

He assumed they passed by invisible doors, access points to rooms or other hallways but there was no way to know for sure. The way the blue light lit up in the ceiling proved that at least the surface of the metal must be transparent. Those who planned to live aboard must've had a method to know where to stop but he detected no marks anywhere as they traveled.

"AI," Hoffner called out. "Direct us to the supply room."

"Affirmative, Captain," Sid replied. "Please follow the green line to your destination."

The light appeared overhead and directed them to continue along. It ended in a wall but as they approached, the surface melted away, granting access to another hallway. Without Sid, getting lost would be too easy. Hoffner checked his tablet and ensured he mapped a way back to the hangar. If something happened, he didn't want to be stuck for too long.

This place is a real maze. Why had the people built it in such a way? Perhaps the design presented a defensive capability. Like old castles with their uneven stairs, only the inhabitants knew them precisely. It tripped up invaders. Such a convoluted layout provided the same type of confusion. Security by design.

Damn inconvenient but I get it. Hoffner glanced back at his men. They seemed uneasy. Any alien contact might've brought the same reaction but this place felt particularly foreign. The allegation they might have encountered a bug race certainly didn't help. Media villainized insects for a long time. Even if the creatures proved benevolent, the human mind was predisposed toward revulsion.

"Captain," Olly's voice piped over his communicator. "How're you doing? Have you located the supplies?"

Hoffner looked ahead and sighed. "I think we're getting close. This place is pretty confusing."

"I'm going to send you a ping so you can get back to us if you have to," Olly replied. A moment later, Hoffner's tablet made a sound and he saw a blip some distance off. "Did you get it?"

"I did. Thanks, Darnell." Hoffner glanced up. They were still following the green line. "We still seem to be moving away from you guys."

"Not a surprise. I think you'll find the supplies near an access point to the engineering section."

"I don't want to get too close to the fabrication thing you talked about," Hoffner said. "Do you know how far off we are from it?"

"It's several decks below us. It would take a lot to stumble on it."

Hoffner nodded. "Glad to hear it. We'll let you know when we find what we're after."

Another several hundred meters later, they came upon another door that melted away, granting them access to a large chamber full of metal crates. They fell in and cleared the room, checking every corner before considering it entirely safe. Sourceless lights beamed overhead, shining down on the glimmering floor and surfaces.

It's unnerving that everything looks like liquid metal. Hoffner frowned. *But this must be the place.*

"AI, can you open these crates?"

"Press the sides and they will open of their own accord. Please note, the contents have been held in a perfect vacuum to protect them from decay. It should be anything you need for further repairs on the ship."

Hoffner knelt beside one and did as he was instructed, pressing near the top of the first crate he came to. The top seemed to melt backwards and vanish into the back, revealing a neatly stacked set of cables and other odd parts he couldn't identify. He checked another before connecting with Olly again.

"We've found at least one supply area. This technology…the way the doors open and the crates work…it's pretty extraordinary."

"That's what we're finding," Olly replied. "Luckily, the internal systems aren't as strange. We're able to make effective changes."

"Do you want us to start bringing this stuff to you?"

"Just catalog it if you can," Olly said. "If it's close to the engineering section, we might need it down there. Once you've got a good reading on all the parts, send it to my tablet and keep looking for another room."

"We're on it." Hoffner turned to his men. "Okay, men. Let's get these open and figure out what's in them. God knows what we'll need and when so don't miss any boxes. You saw how I opened it. Get to it. We're on a tight schedule here."

Hoffner was happy they had something to do. Standing around in the hangar gave men time to think. A little busy work would keep them occupied. The last thing they needed was idle chatter and worry. Morale suffered from that kind of thing and he couldn't afford it. Not on an alien vessel in the middle of a battle zone with other alien vessels bent on their destruction.

Just another day in the corps, I guess. Let's just hope it's not our last.

Chapter 10

The Behemoth followed the Silver Star for nearly fifteen minutes, heading into the empty space between Mars and Earth. Their pursuers maintained a sizable distance but did not falter. Gray wondered what exactly they were waiting for and why they hadn't engaged again. Maybe they needed a minute to evaluate their enemy.

I doubt those jerks are surprised often. Gray watched his tablet and observed various reports across the ship. Fighters were refueled and ready for launch. He had a few ideas of how to prolong the fight, to give his men aboard the Silver Star the time they needed. How many tricks he could employ remained to be seen.

"Sir, the enemies are picking up speed," Paul's voice brought Gray out of his thoughts. "They seem to be ready for another bout."

Gray tapped the com and hooked up with Revente. "I need you to launch the fighters and have them slow those bastards down."

"How do you mean? Our weapons can't penetrate their shields."

"Nor have they launched any of their own fighters yet," Gray replied. "I'm sure they've got them and they'll come out soon. If they have any regard for their people, they'll have to provide support. That will give us what we need to keep out of their reach. We're buying time here, Estaban and I need your help."

"We could try the bombers again," Revente offered.

Gray shook his head. "No, they've already proven they can knock the projectiles out before they get close. We'd be putting a lot of pilots at risk for nothing. What we need is fast and agile. Get those jockeys out there and let them do what they do best. Nip at the heels."

"Okay, we'll do what we can."

"Keep sending your report feeds to the bridge."
Gray killed the connection. "Are they trying for weapon
lock, Paul?"

"Negative, sir. I'm not reading any locks."

"Redding, do we have range?"

"Extreme," Redding replied. "I *might* be able to
take a pot shot but at this distance, evasive wouldn't be
hard. Turn a direct hit into a graze…and that's all they
have to do."

"Understood. If they close within medium range,
something we can guarantee a direct hit with, tell me
right away. I want to keep stabbing at them."

"Perhaps we need to turn to the offensive," Clea
said. "It would not be expected."

"Nor are we entirely ready," Gray replied. "Two
against one…no. We need an advantage in that fight and
right now, the Silver Star isn't providing it."

"Sir, I'm reading a debris net coming up
starboard," Tim said. "Looks like civilian crews marked it
for clean up next week."

"What kind of debris?" Gray asked. "Natural?"

"Seems to be the fall out of some kind of mining operation. A fair sized asteroid was here and they broke it up." Tim took a moment to finish reading. "I'm reading rocks and spent supplies from the operation. It's just waiting for a recycling run."

"How big is it?" Everly asked.

"One point five kilometers around," Paul replied. "They really gathered a lot of crap. Wow, I bet *that* job's boring."

Gray smiled.

"What're you considering?" Clea said.

"Something like a mine field," Gray replied, clicking over to Revente. "We've got some debris up ahead. Can you see it on your scans?"

"Yes, I've got it."

"Do you think your pilots can take care of that net?"

"For what purpose?"

"I'd like to give our friends a gift," Gray said. "If we can spread it behind us, I'm pretty sure it'll provide some decent camouflage."

"Won't their shields deflect it?"

"Yes, but I'm not done. We'll jettison a few pulse bombs into the mess but not too many. I don't want them picking up the weapon signature in their scans. When they get close, we'll remote detonate and see if that doesn't give them the bloody nose we're hoping for."

Revente hesitated for several moments but finally replied. "Okay, I like it. We're on it."

"Be sure they open the net then spread the stuff but not too thin or it won't cover up the bombs."

"You think it'll work?" Clea asked.

"Depends on what result you're after," Gray turned to her. "If you're asking do I think it'll blow one of them up, no, I don't. But I do believe it'll make them be cautious and again, buy us some time."

"Clever."

"I go easy on you when we play chess." Gray turned to Redding. "Make sure you get us closer to the Silver Star. Keep your distance from the net. This is one of those things where you only have one shot to get it right and those pilots will definitely need us out of the way."

***

Meagan and Panther wing raced away from the Behemoth, preparing for a guerrilla battle. They'd practiced harassment techniques plenty of times before in war games with the Behemoth. She remembered grueling hours spent dodging weapon lock and blasting away with quarter power shots at the delicate parts of their targets.

This will be no different. It's a phrase she used on her pilots just before they launched again but she barely believed it herself. Live fire always made things different. The Behemoth wanted them to learn a lesson, not obliterate them from the sky. Anyone who didn't take it seriously needed to do so now.

"Panther One, this is Giant Control, come in." Revente's voice filled her helmet.

"Panther One here. What's going on?"

"I need Panthers One through Four to disengage your current mission and high tail it back toward the Behemoth."

"With all due respect, sir, why? I don't want to leave half my wing out here without me."

"Don't worry, you're just carrying out a quick task before returning to the fray. We need as many fighters distracting the enemy as we can." Revente paused a moment. "I think you'll like what they have in mind anyway."

"I'd better because taking off doesn't feel right." Meagan switched the channel to the other ships in her wing. "Looks like we've got a side game, guys. I need two, three and four to form up on me. The rest of you engage as we discussed. Work with Tiger Wing to really give them hell."

Meagan pulled up and spun around with the other three ships in tow. She patched back in with Giant Control "Okay, we're on our way back. What's so damn important?"

"There's a net full of debris near the ship. Roughly a kilometer in radius so plenty of garbage. We're going to jettison a couple pulse bombs. You're going to spread out the rubbish and plant the ordinance in the middle."

Meagan nodded. "I see. So why does it take four of us?"

"The net's secure with a magnetic clamp with a coded lock. We don't have time to decrypt it. Two of you will attach tow cables to the net. One will blow the lock. You'll then open the contents and drag it across the flight path of the enemies. A couple extra shots should get it moving and you can contain it to a tight spread with the net."

"And the Pulse Bombs?"

"Panther Four will drop them amongst the trash, leaving them to float around. As soon as you're finished, I want you to get the hell out of the way. Back toward the Behemoth. I'm warning all wings about what we're planning because when the enemy ships reach a threshold, they have to disengage and take the long way around to get back us."

"Okay, we're on it." Meagan briefed her wing on their objective and how they'd take care of it. Mick, Panther Two, spoke up.

"That clamp they're talking about is pretty small and if we blast it, that might cause the whole net to fly off. It's going to be pretty damn heavy."

"Good," Meagan replied. "We'll get into position so when the clamp goes, we'll use the momentum from the shot to drag the contents to where we need them. Panther Four, keep those pulse bombs as far away from shooting as you can."

"I don't fancy being turned into molten slag," Shelly, Panther Four, replied. "Don't worry. I'll treat them with more respect than the bomber guys do."

"Hey," David, Panther Three said, "they drop them on valuable targets. I'd call that pretty respectful."

Meagan grinned but didn't fuel their fun. "Let's focus on the task, people. Panther Two and I will attach our cables. Three, you're on shooting detail."

The net loomed ahead, a massive blob of junk both natural and manmade. Without environmental shields, such debris could obliterate a ship, tearing through the hull and causing no end of damage. Cleanup crews from Earth cataloged sites with excessive rock or garbage left from mining operations and sent people to take care of them.

Gathering them up allowed ships to note their locations and avoid running into them. Once there was enough, a recycling ship would make the rounds, gathering it all up and returning to Earth to repurpose the stuff. Agile ships needed to collect the pieces, larger ones carted it away.

Mick was right about it being heavy. Two wasps might have a hard time pulling it all. Luckily, they'd be leaving some behind, essentially just pulling the net aside and allowing momentum to carry it all. Without the shot giving it a jolt, they'd probably need all four ships to pull it anywhere.

And even then, they'd be flying slow.

"Panther Two, I'll be on top." Meagan paused. "Don't you *dare* make a joke about that."

"Wouldn't dream of it, Panther One," Mick chuckled, dropping below her vessel and angling his own to line up the tow cable with the net. "In position."

Meagan followed suit on the opposite side. They fired their tow cables, catching the net well above and below the clamps, far enough away that any damage incurred wouldn't destroy their connection. She throttled her wench and felt the tug on her ship. A tiny jostle indicated Mick made his shot as well.

Panther Three settled in between them and took aim. "Get ready, guys," David called out. "I'm going to take three shots total to get the stuff moving."

Three flashes lit up the world behind Meagan and a moment later she felt the tension in her line go slack as the net opened wide. "Here we go," she called to Mick. "Throttle up and under."

"On it."

They pulled away, opening the throttles as they tore the net free and dragged what little debris along which clung to the surface. Meagan turned to look at their pursuers, still a long distance off but menacingly close in reality. They needed to establish the trap quickly so they'd be nowhere near the blast but more importantly, they didn't want to tip off their enemy to the plan.

Panther Four approached carrying the bombs and deposited them amongst the trash while One and Two continued to pull. "Get ready to detach," Meagan said, checking her scanner to ensure they'd covered as much of the area as possible. "On my mark. Three...two...one...now!"

She hit the button and her cable came free. Mick followed suit and the two of them regrouped with Three and Four. "Make your way back toward the Behemoth, full speed. Panther wing, give yourself another twenty seconds of action then get moving. Rendezvous with the Behemoth ASAP."

A series of acknowledgements came through the com. Meagan checked her rear camera and wondered if the ploy would work. Did the trap have a chance to work? Would it leave the enemy reeling? She had faith in Captain Atwell. His tactic, unorthodox as it may've seemed, sure sounded like a good idea.

Even if it didn't cripple an enemy vessel, it might make them cautious and so far, they knew caution was not the strength of these invaders. They liked to drive in, punching and swinging with everything they had. Overwhelming their opposition with deadly, brutal force. Subtlety seemed totally alien to them but they were about to learn a really hard lesson.

One Meagan was more than happy to help teach.

Chapter 11

"The trap is set," Paul announced. "The fighters have positioned the debris, and the bomb, in the path of the enemy. I've got a good reading on the device and can detonate at any time."

"Perfect." Gray patted his knees. "Keep us moving, Redding. Make it look like we're trying to run away."

"Sir?" Redding glanced over her shoulder.

"You know…make it look…" Gray shrugged. "Frantic."

"Fly…frantically, sir?"

"Just put some feeling into it."

Redding nodded slowly and turned back to her console. "Aye, sir. Adding feeling now."

Clea cracked a smile at Gray. "I suspect that works better on smaller vessels, sir."

"Maybe. But every little bit of thought helps," Gray replied. "Have you ever heard the expression 'the power of positive thinking'?"

"Yes, I believe it is used by charlatans trying to sell things which do not work."

"She's got you there, sir," Everly said. "I'm getting a report from the fighters. They are preparing to disengage."

"Why are we not letting them continue the fight?" Clea asked. "Won't it seem suspicious that they're suddenly breaking away?"

"Based on what little we know of the enemy's tactics, there are two things they might be thinking about us," Gray explained. "Either we're total cowards and we'll throw our people away to save our own skins or we're struck dumb with compassion, which means we'll toss aside the distraction to save our people. Whatever direction they take, they feel they have the upper hand with us."

"That makes a certain kind of sense."

"Of course it does." Gray grinned. "Now, sit back and watch the fireworks. Our next tactic may not be so well received…or well played for that matter."

Unlike fighter combat, large ship board battles required patience. Everything moved slower and the stakes were dramatically higher. A good blast from something like the Behemoth could cripple an enemy vessel and possibly destroy it. The trick came down to weakening the shields enough to do catastrophic damage.

Combat defenses made environmental shields look like tissue paper. Clea made it clear when she briefed them long ago. Properly calibrated protection could allow two ships to batter each other for hours if not days. One popular theory suggested this was why the enemy always sent two ships. Even the best shields could not stand up to a barrage from multiple vessels.

"Five minutes until the enemy is in range," Paul said. "They are still gaining speed and our fighters have disengaged."

"ETA for their arrival here?" Everly asked.

"Three minutes. They're taking the long way around our little mine field."

"Why didn't we drop more?" Tim turned to the captain. "We could've put in enough to wipe out both ships."

"Too many bombs would've picked up on their scanners," Clea said. "Pulse munitions emit a distinct signature. Two amongst so much debris will simply appear like radiation on scanners, the exact kind you would see anywhere in space where objects clung together."

"Oh...that makes sense." Tim turned back to his console. "So they can't pick them out of the junk."

"Correct." Clea confirmed.

"Two minutes." Paul announced. "Our ships are docking in the hangars."

Gray nodded. "When we have everyone on board, I want you to speed up, Redding. Overtake the Silver Star if you have to. Make it look like we're going to make a real run for it. That'll get them moving."

Clea stiffened with realization. "Causing them to be less cautious so they'll run right into your little trap."

"By the time their scans pick up the two bombs, it'll be way too late."

"Sixty seconds to optimal range." Paul paused. "Sir, they're not slowing down."

"They'll barrel right through the trap," Everly said. "Get ready to detonate."

"When the bombs are closest to the shields, Paul," Gray added, "hit the button."

"Aye, sir." Paul watched his console intently, waiting for a series of numbers to hit zero. The others stared at the view screen, set to the rear cameras. They watched the enemy vessels power toward them, moving haphazardly fast, unconcerned about the debris field in their way. Tiny flashes of green light indicated where the first of the debris burned up on contact with their shields.

Paul held up his hand. "Detonating…now!" He slammed a finger down on the console and the screen lit up with a massive white flash, engulfing both targets in an instant. Tim, Redding and Agatha cheered but Gray shushed them with a quick gesture. It took nearly ten seconds for the light to fade from the bombs going off.

When it did, the enemy vessels had stopped but they remained intact. Smoke came out of the one nearest the blast, seemingly from extensive damage in the lower levels on the port side. Gray leaned back and let out a sigh. He had allowed himself to hope they'd do more but this seemed to be enough for now.

"Can you get a reading on the damage?" Everly asked.

"One ship experienced only minor damage to their port side. Their shields held strong in the blast and it's still at...eighty percent capacity."

"And the other?"

"Shields are currently down," Paul replied. "Extensive damage to the lower levels. I'm picking up a hull breach. I can't get anymore."

"That's enough." Gray rubbed his chin, watching as the relatively undamaged ship moved between them and the damaged craft. This might be the time to turn and attack. "They're on the defensive."

"Which is usually when an animal is at its most dangerous," Clea answered.

"You said I should attack when they weren't hurt," Gray replied, "and now you're cautioning me?"

"They wouldn't have expected it before," Clea said. "Now…they're ready for us to turn around. Without shields, you're right, we could take down that ship but they'll use their shielded friend as cover and we'll still be up against twice as many guns as we have."

"I don't know if they're going to fall for another trick."

"They don't know tricks, Captain. I believe the plan was to get the Silver Star operational enough to get their story." Clea nodded to him. "You proved to me that we should stick to it."

Gray nodded. "I agree. Redding, catch us up to the Silver Star and have them change course. I want to loop around and get between those two ships and Earth. Time to go back to being the shield. Paul, get Olly on the line. I want to know where they are with the repairs and how long we can expect to wait. There's still a lot of work to do, people. Let's get it done."

***

The explosion made the marines high five each other and hoot enthusiastically. The others didn't quite share their enthusiasm but they definitely seemed glad it worked. For Olly's part, he wondered how long their little victory would last. Surprises like that only worked once. They'd be a lot more cautious in the future and maybe that's what Captain Atwell wanted.

Olly finished briefing the Behemoth on where they were. He knew they wanted better than his ambiguous ETA but his crew hadn't finished mapping the extent of damage. Captain Atwell tasked him with restoring weapon capabilities, to help even the odds.

They made progress, however, especially with gathering some context into the people who built the ship. If Cathleen's reboot worked, they might gain some insight into their way of thinking. Such a point would go a long way toward understanding why they structured their tech the way they did.

Maria finished mapping conduits and after twenty minutes of rerouting, managed to get power to several systems. Some were still damaged, including the computer specifically designed to wake the inhabitants of the pods up. Gregory joined them and started to see what he could do with it.

"Lieutenant," Lisa called. "I'd like to get to the bridge to see what I can do. If I can direct connect into their systems there, I might make some headway with the databases."

"We should send someone to engineering as well," Maria added. "If we work in tandem, we'll get a lot more done."

"Take an escort," Olly said, "and check in every ten minutes. But I agree…though we seem to have pretty solid access to various systems down here."

"AI," Lisa looked up as she spoke, "please give us the blue line to engineering and the ship's bridge."

"When you leave the room, take a left for the bridge and a right for engineering. You will need to use an elevator to reach both. The former is above us by several decks and the other down and near the fabrication facility."

"Is this a good idea?" Lisa's escort asked before they left. She'd learned his name was Chuck, a newer addition to the marines. He didn't sound scared, just cautious. She smiled at him.

"I'm sure it'll be no big deal. All the internal security stuff is off. We'll be fine."

"Famous last words," Chuck muttered. "Alright, let's move out."

Maria also headed off and just as they cleared the door, Cathleen clapped her hands, calling out, "Lieutenant! I'm into that database! Sid is translating it right now."

"Amazing," Olly replied. "Have it put the information on my console over here."

"Linking it up now." Lisa hummed. "It seems to be a fragment of history...their time stamps don't make any sense though."

Olly expected a string of text, something translated into English to make it easier to read. Instead, a video popped up first displaying a major city from a high altitude then zooming in to various parts. It showed the inhabitants after a moment who looked remarkably human but for a few key differences.

First, most of them sported odd colored hair which didn't appear naturally on Earth. Deep reds, vibrant blues, lime green mixed in with the occasional raven black. Skin tone ranged from pale to tinged with gold and silver. They seemed to glow under the white-gold light of their sun.

Olly hoped it might give him the composition of their atmosphere and radiation levels from their star but this seemed to be a historical document, not scientific.

People milled about, performing everyday tasks as they traveled the city which reminded him much of New York. Congested streets housed hundreds of people and sleek vehicles which tugged along sluggishly behind endless lines of others. Without sound, he couldn't immediately tell what was going on. Was this business as usual or did something happen to make travel so slow?

Then he noticed the looks on people's faces. Panic. They weren't going to work, they were trying to evacuate. A few moments later, the sky lit up and huge blasts pummeled the buildings around the people he watched. Rubble tumbled from the highest skyscraper, crushing people and vehicles under enormous weight.

The aerial bombardment didn't seem like it would stop any time soon and Olly had no interest in watching thousands of people die. "AI, fast forward, please. Take me to the part where people boarded this ship."

The video stopped and a moment later picked up in a wilderness setting. Twisted, white and red trees stretched into the sky. A green stream passed over jagged rocks. Fluffy gray clouds littered the teal sky. As the camera panned over the wilderness, it settled on the ship landed in an open area miles long but surrounded by trees.

"They hid it there," Sid announced, "because the foliage defended it against the active scans of the enemy. They targeted technological hubs first and by the time they resorted to this ship, few places remained. The secret of Protocol Seven came too late."

Men and women boarded the ship, some carrying belongings, others unburdened. The view changed to the hallways Olly and his people walked down recently until it settled on the chambers. People embraced, some cried and some bitterly approached their pods without a word. Each crawled in and the tube sealed up, putting them into their deep slumber.

"They look like us," Cathleen said, "for the most part."

Olly nodded. "And they boarded their version of the Ark, hoping for a better world when they weathered the storm. How the hell did they break atmosphere and escape the enemy?"

"That information is currently locked. I cannot access it at this time."

Olly rolled his eyes. "Thanks, AI. I'll get that from you later." He turned to Cathleen. "Was this everything in that database?"

Cathleen nodded. "But I think it gave me an access point to the next one. I'll start digging at it."

"Good. Let me know how you do." Olly patched his com to Lisa and Maria. "Hey, we need to get weapons back online ASAP. That's your first priority. Lisa, when you get to the bridge, I want to know whether we can take control of navigation. Find out. We might need the Behemoth to send someone over to fly this thing."

"AI seems to be doing a pretty good job right now," Lisa replied.

"Why thank you, Lieutenant Oxton," Sid said, "but intuitive flying beats computer flying any day. My people learned that years ago."

"You heard the um...man." Olly cleared his throat. "Anyway, those are the priorities. Weapons, manual flight, database access. Everyone on board?"

He received a line of acknowledgement and turned back to his own task. They were still a ways off but closer than ever before. With context into the enemy and what they could do, he figured he had all the incentive in the world to fight and really push hard to get this work done. Just before diving back in, he sent the video to the Behemoth for them to review.

If anyone doubted the danger of the threat they faced, they wouldn't for long.

Chapter 12

Clea finished watching the video Olly sent and turned to Gray. His expression remained grave throughout his viewing and when the screen went dark, he drew a deep breath. She understood his concern. Unlike him, she'd seen this type of thing before on other worlds. Her own people picked up the pieces of other cultures devastated by the enemy.

This was Earth's first real look at what they faced if they failed.

"I can't believe…they attacked civilian targets…" Gray shook his head.

"That's how they operate," Clea replied. "The stakes are high, Captain. If we fail, your world suffers the ultimate price."

"I'm getting that." Gray rubbed his eyes. "We seem to be doing okay so far."

Clea smirked but it lacked all humor. "I will remain cautiously optimistic, isn't that the term?"

Gray nodded. "Yes…and good point."

"Captain," Paul practically shouted with alarm. "Captain, the enemy! They've…they've disappeared!"

"What?" Gray stood. "What do you mean *disappeared*?"

"They're gone! Straight off my scans!" Paul gestured helplessly at the controls. "I have no idea how it's possible but…there you are."

"You're not finished." Everly scowled. "Keep looking. They have to be out there somewhere."

"Maybe they did a hyperjump," Redding offered. "We did some serious damage to one of their ships after all. They probably bugged out."

"They had one fully operational ship and another still combat effective," Clea said. "They did *not* simply abandon their operation."

"There's something to be said about Redding's assessment," Everly added. "Paul, do a search for any hyperjump activity. If they did it, they had to leave a wake, right?"

"I'm not picking anything up…" Paul hummed. "No, nothing odd at all."

"Tim, what've we got as far as solar bodies in the area?" Gray leaned on the young man's seat to look at his screen. "Anything bigger than the garbage we picked up?"

"Um…prospectors identified an asteroid nearby." Tim shrugged. "It's pretty big. Large mineral deposits. They were planning an operation in the next few weeks."

"Big enough to hide behind?"

"Not the Behemoth but it could easily hide a wing of fighters. Especially if they stayed tightly grouped."

Gray turned to Everly. "Have Revente launch a wing and get them behind that asteroid."

"What's your thought?"

"I think it's their turn for a trick and the only thing we can do is hope we can counter it."

Everly got on the com to get the fighters going. Gray returned to his seat, leaning forward. Clea watched him for a long moment, wondering exactly what he considered at times like that. How did he strategize against the unknown? Her own people found it quite the challenge. Creative as they were, they struggled in fights like this.

The humans seemed to thrive in them. As they waited for the enemy to spring their attack, they remained outwardly calm, doing their jobs to the best of their abilities. That was one of the things Clea liked most about them. They met challenges without allowing the weight of consequence to effect their performance.

Her people could learn a great deal from them. She sure had.

"Fighters away, Captain," Everly announced. "They'll be in position in less than two minutes."

"Good." Gray checked his tablet. "Give us some distance on the Silver Star, Redding. I don't want to end up in her aft if something goes awry."

Redding ran her hand along the screen and engaged the retro thrusters, reducing speed. The Silver Star pulled ahead of them, crawling to a respectable distance. Clea squinted at the screen, watching for anything out of the ordinary. Shimmering stars, a ripple in space, or even a flash of light might provide an early warning of what might come.

Tension built. Clea felt like they were being watched by a great predator hiding in the bushes about to pounce. She clenched her fist in anticipation. *Where are you?* Alliance engagements tended to be straightforward. The enemy attacked and one side or the other was repelled. These cat and mouse games were new to her.

"Contact!" Paul shouted. "Port side!"

"What the hell?" Everly leaned half forward as the enemy ships seemed to appear from nowhere a short distance away. Clea estimated they must've been no more than two hundred kilometers off, about as far as when they passed by them during their initial engagement. "Open fire!"

The order came too late as the enemy weapons flashed.

"Brace for impact!" Gray grabbed his seat as he shouted. Clea tensed and a moment later, the entire ship shook from the blasts. Lights flickered on the bridge. Agatha shouted and Redding worked her controls, moving her hands rapidly though what she was trying to do, Clea couldn't guess.

"Evasive!" Gray grunted. "Get us out of their line of fire!"

The ship jostled as Redding took them downward, a rapid maneuver that pressed everyone into their seats. Clea envisioned that people lost their footing throughout the ship, collapsing under the sudden change of velocity and course. Tim gripped his console tightly and Paul worked his controls rapidly.

"Return fire," Everly barked. "Give them a reason to back the hell off!"

Their own weapons caused the ship to vibrate as they returned fire. No lock but a few direct hits splashed against the enemy's shields. The bombardment continued and they saw a group of enemy fighters rushing out from behind their carriers, rushing toward the Behemoth at breakneck speed. They were triangular with fins on the top and bottom housing weapons that lit up space.

"Get our fighters in here now!" Everly continued giving the orders. "Engage! Engage!"

Gray turned to Paul. "Damage report?"

"Still coming in, sir!" Paul shook his head. "I've got an overload of data and we're still being bombarded! Shields dropped for a moment but they're holding now. We took a direct hit on decks seven and eight. Hull breach has been sealed with automatic repair systems. Engine power has dropped to eighty percent!"

Another blast shook the ship and Gray nearly fell out of his seat. "Redding, I thought I told you to get us out of here!"

"I'm on it, sir! This thing isn't exactly a fighter! We're moving as fast as we can."

"Fighters have engaged!" Tim reported. "They're distracting the enemy pilots."

"They're powering up for another full barrage!" Paul shouted. "Sir, we can't take another *full* on attack on the port side!"

"Twist us, Redding," Gray said, "give them another angle to beat on."

Clea turned to her tablet and read the damage reports from the enemy. The one hit with the bombs restored their shields to a little more than fifty percent. Their weapons were sure online. They powered up for another attack. The Behemoth's shots hit enough to give her some hope but if the two enemies fired at the same time…

"Ms Redding," Clea said. "Get us in position with one of the enemy ships between us and the other. They're both powering up again and if each shoot at us…well, like Ensign Bailey said, we cannot take that."

"No pressure or anything," Redding muttered, stabbing her console with quick motions. The ship moved again, this time in a more erratic manner. Something deep in the hull groaned from the effort before the ship suddenly plunged downward and starboard, away from the enemies entirely. "Hold on!"

She hit a button and the fusion drive lit up and the engines roared. The enemy fired but they weren't there, a clean miss! Paul checked his scans and hooted. "Only one of them is facing us now and we're giving them our starboard!"

"Calm down," Gray commanded. "This isn't remotely over. Redding, keep fire on those bastards and push us to catch up with the Silver Star. Paul, get them on the line and see what they can do to help. This outnumbered nonsense needs to end now."

***

Meagan's Panther Wing and Tiger Wing launched again and took position near the asteroid, close enough to mask their scan signatures. Each of their fighters remained close enough to see the other pilots in their cockpits, enough to wave at one another. This sortie didn't even have a briefing. Just a note to get out there and hide behind the asteroid.

Revente warned them to maintain radio silence. They communicated in scan pings, a military code which conveyed an impressively large vocabulary. Even those they kept to a minimum. In the event of an order, Meagan prepared a message to have them fall out. If they had to fight, they'd break silence.

Until then, they waited.

Meagan hadn't been in a fighter for such a lengthy period of time since first boarding the Behemoth. During their initial training and drills, they spent hours in their fighters, launching and docking, practicing rapid deployments. Things slacked off somewhat for a while but they maintained their edge with surprise mock combat engagements.

Even when they'd be woken up every other night to board their ships and get out into space, Meagan didn't feel the tension she did now. Revente wouldn't have had them launch without a good reason. It dawned on her she didn't see the enemy ships and a chill ran down her spine.

If they fled, we wouldn't be out here right now. Meagan looked over her shoulder and in every direction she could. *Where the hell are they then?*

They appeared out of nowhere, weapons blazing. "Holy shit!" One of the pilots broke radio silence but Meagan couldn't blame him. This was unexpected in a major way. *How? What kind of technology allowed...well...that?!*

Fighters deployed from one of their hangars, heading away toward the Silver Star. Weapons tore at the Behemoth and they returned fire. The combat started wild and didn't seem like it would slow down any time soon. This might very well be the deciding battle, the one where one side or another wouldn't walk away.

"Form up on me," Meagan spoke into her com, pulling back the stick on her fighter and jamming the throttle to full. "Engage those fighters. Keep them away from the Silver Star."

Mick came on the line. "Readings indicate they're armed similar to us. Shields, pulse cannons…possible radiation from projectile ordinance."

"I'm reading fifteen," David said. "No, scratch that. I'm seeing twenty."

"Quite the discrepancy." Mick joked. "You missed five of them?"

"Hey, they're tightly grouped!"

Meagan strained against the g force of her fighter pushing top speed, her muscles tense. The enemy loomed ahead but they didn't even acknowledge their pursuers. *Why do they want the Silver Star so badly?* Could that be why they came to Earth again? Were they after the alien ship? *Makes sense…but I don't have time for speculation*.

"If they're going to give us their aft, oblige them with some well placed shots, ladies and gentlemen," Meagan spoke over the com. "Let's do this."

A flash of light made her wince from the left. David must've taken the first shot, a pulse blast that lit up space and grazed one of the fighters. Before anyone else in the wing could pull the trigger, the enemy ships decided to change course, flipping around to meet the Behemoth fighters head on.

"That's more like it," Shelly called out. "Let's do this!"

"Stick with your wingman and play it by the numbers!" Meagan replied. "Here we go!"

Meagan and Mick pulled up and to the left while Panthers Three and Four went right. The rest of the wing dove and weaved about, spreading out the potential conflict to give them some room to maneuver. Each group of two pulled a contingent of the enemy, between two and three though the Behemoth crew outnumbered the enemy fighters.

We've got this. Meagan spoke the words to herself as she juked right to avoid a pulse blast. It whizzed by her ship, just skimming her shields. "This guy's all over me, Mick." Another couple shots missed but it was only a matter of time. "How're you doing?"

"Mine's pretty persistent too but," Mick spun his fighter in a barrel roll and dove, striking the breaks so he spun, his aft spinning down to line up a shot. He pulled the trigger and his pursuer erupted in a ball of blue then winked out, destroyed. "I had a plan."

"Nice maneuver," Meagan grunted as she pulled to the left and lowered her throttle. Retro thrusters engaged in her front and the enemy nearly collided with her. Apparently, he had some sense of self preservation because he pulled up and flew past her, wildly dodging to avoid a lock. *You're screwed now, buddy*.

The HUD in her cockpit lit up as the enemy danced near her reticle. She moved the stick with perfect finesse, lining the shot up for her computer to get a solid lock. The computer pinged a monotonous rhythm then suddenly emitted a solid buzz. Meagan pulled the trigger, her cockpit warming instantly as the pulse blasters annihilated her target.

"Watch it!" Meagan had no idea whose voice shouted over the line or if it was even meant for her but she reacted, pulling to the right. The ship strained at the sudden maneuver and even with the inertial dampeners, her vision blackened temporarily. A missile flew by so close she could make out the fins surrounding the thruster in the back.

The ordinance exploded a moment later and Meagan gunned her throttle to avoid the concussion wake. Her attacker, a ship trying to maneuver for another shot, flew nearby in the opposite direction. She adjusted course, making a play to gain the same advantage he sought.

Chaos raged around them as ships dodged and weaved, climbing and banking in an effort to pull off shots. Distraction tended to be the biggest danger of space combat. The temptation to attack another, easier to target craft always entered the equation. Meagan constantly hammered into her pilots the importance of spacial awareness: always focus on the thing that's focusing on you.

In this case, her opponent had it in for her, of that she was certain. He already took one shot and wouldn't give up. She spun her craft and took a pot shot, something to throw him off guard. His ship bounced away, an incredible maneuver that made her head spin.

How'd you even do that? His thrusters essentially tossed him a few feet to the right, a quick burst from the side moving him to safety.

He returned the favor, firing several blasts in her direction. Meagan dodged, turning her craft sideways to fly between his attacks. The pulse beams sizzled against her shields but she took no damage.

They began flying directly at one another and she returned fire, letting a missile fly to distract him from shooting back. He once again pulled off a stupendous maneuver, climbing out of her path and narrowly avoiding destruction from the missile. As he leveled out, Meagan moved in behind him with a perfect shot at his aft.

Now I've got you. Meagan hit the computer and tried for another lock but her opponent's erratic motion made the computer useless. She eyeballed it, taking several shots that he dodged about like a fly avoiding a swatter. *Who the hell am I fighting? Their version of the Red Baron?*

Meagan fired again and this time, the enemy dropped below her attack and suddenly spun in place. As he came around, his weapons discharged, blasting her with a direct hit. The fighter bounced from the initial contact and she lost control for a moment, careening away from the fight and back toward a large fray of combat.

"I've been hit," she announced, trying to keep the stress from her voice. "Checking systems."

All the calm she could muster didn't fight off the anxiety of knowing the incredible pilot was still out there, still trying to take her out. He might already be behind her but she didn't have scans to prove it. Power fluctuated then the automatic backup system came online. She saw her nemesis had indeed moved in behind her and was seeking a lock.

The flight stick didn't respond at first but as the engines fired back up, she was able to jam her controls starboard and pull away. Hitting full throttle, she saw pulse blasts zing by her cockpit, missing by mere inches. Damage reports indicated her shields were at thirty percent, not enough to stop another direct hit. They were charging but she needed a good minute for them to be effective again.

Don't have time for that. "Where the hell are you, Mick?" Meagan asked over the com. "This guy is all over me!"

"I've got my own problems," he replied, "but I'm working my way back to you. Hey, I've got an idea."

"I'm all for them."

"Remember those retro videos? The Blue Angels?"

Meagan dodged, grunting at the effort. Once again, she narrowly avoided death. "Get to the point, man!"

"If your sensors are up, I'm coming straight at you. We have to make this close…I'm thinking no more than three meters."

"What's no more than three meters?"

"The distance we'll be from one another as we pass by. You dive, I'll climb. Our friends will have a quick meeting they hopefully won't walk away from."

"Jesus…" Meagan nodded. "Sounds insane but I'm in."

"Ten seconds."

That's a lifetime out here…more than enough time for this jerk to put me down.

"Count it down," Meagan glanced over her shoulder. Her guy was closing in. *What the hell? Need the up close kill or are you finally realizing I'm too wily for your bad shooting?*

Shields read fifty percent. *At least I won't die if he gets a lucky shot but two pulse beams will do me in.* She spun, a barrel roll dodge which took her slightly off course. Her sensors showed how to correct and she nudged herself back into position.

"We still good?" She asked Mick.

"You should see me. Get ready!"

Mick appeared suddenly ahead of her and if not for the precise measurements of their sensors, she would've sworn they were about to collide. Trusting in their instruments went against her every instinct. When

he went by, she felt his wake and she pressed her flight
stick forward, entering a swift dive.

Light erupted behind her and on her scan, she
saw the enemy ships collided, turning into a ball of blue
light then fading to nothing.

"Oh my God, that actually worked!" Meagan
allowed herself some relief. "Good job, Mick!"

"Goes to show they don't have the same
communication network we do," Mick replied. "Looks like
they're all out here independently. "

"Good point." Meagan looked down and frowned
at the readings on her console. The containment unit
holding her pulse engine had a hairline crack. Any more
damage might rip it open and then, she'd be done. Even
if the shields prevented a full on destructive blow, a
pulse breach meant certain death.

"I'm in a little more trouble. Look at these
readings."

"Just be careful," Mick replied. "I've done an
entire mission with a cracked core. It's cool. We're
almost done here."

The enemy fighters had been depleted but so had they. Half of Tiger wing was down. Lieutenant Richard Martin, Panther Seven, wasn't responding to hails. This was a real fight, the kind they'd trained for, sure but no one knew just how bad it would get or how deadly. Meagan took a deep breath and steadied herself for the rest of the engagement.

Far off, she saw the larger ships still battering at each other. The Behemoth leveraged a lot of punishment on their enemies but they got as good as they gave. Their larger weapons required some recharge time so it wasn't constant but every blast made the entire sector light up like a star passed by. How much punishment could either side take before folding?

"Let's get back in there, Mick. I sure hope they've got a plan on the Behemoth because I sure don't see a good path forward."

"I'm sure they know what they're doing." Mick took the lead. "Now, follow *my* six this time. I'll get us home."

Meagan grinned. "Lead on, my friend. Lead on."

Act 3:

Chapter 13

"Chief Engineer Higgins is on the line," Agatha shouted over the noise on the bridge. "He states damage crews are circulating through the ship, prioritizing damage."

They pressed forward, moving out of the firing arc of the enemy but it was only a temporary saving grace. Auxiliary fired at the enemy, turrets meant to fend off fighters or harass a larger vessel. The enemy returned the shots and even those less powerful weapons caused superficial damage to the Behemoth.

Gray slapped his tablet and brought engineering online. "Higgins, get our shields back up! We can't survive this engagement for long."

"We're working on it, sir!" Higgins voice crackled on the line. "They really did a number on us with that initial foray!"

Gray stood and paced over to Redding's station, peering at her screen. "Can you get us out of here?"

"They have my engines at sixty percent." Redding shrugged. "I can go to maximum speed but it won't be enough to escape."

"Better to be chased than dead. Get us going."

"I can't push it too far or the pulse drive might not take it."

Gray nodded. "Do what you can." He turned to Paul. "Put the Silver Star online. They need to understand the gravity of the situation."

"Report from the fighters," Everly said. "They state the enemy squadron is down to twenty percent effectiveness. They're mopping up now."

"Finally, some good news." Gray rubbed his eyes. "Tell them to wrap it up and be ready for another attack. God knows if they've got more waiting in the rafters."

"Some of them have to come in for repairs," Everly replied. "They're requesting landing clearance."

"Not right now. They're safer out there." Gray checked his tablet as another blast shook the ship. "Redding!"

"I'm on it, sir!"

Agatha cleared her throat. "I've got Lieutenant Darnell on the line."

"Olly," Gray called out. "I hope you've got some good news for us. We're reaching the eleventh hour."

The lights flickered as another blast grazed their shields. Gray clenched his fist and waited for the briefing of the tech crew. *At least Redding dodged that one. How many more before they've put us down? You'd better have something, Olly. For all our sakes.*

***

Prior to the Battle

Olly answered his com, linking up with Lisa. "I'm here. Are you on the bridge?"

"Yes, sir. I've made it and let me tell you, this is a technological paradise." Lisa patched her camera to his tablet and gave him a look. Like the rest of the ship, the walls, floor and ceiling were comprised of the same shimmering, silver metal. A massive black screen dominated one surface across from some chairs with consoles bulging out of the smooth terrain.

"True to the form of the ship at least," Olly replied. "Do you have power up there?"

"I do. I've coordinated with Maria. The good news is all connections are online up here but they can't all link to their services. Those are what she's going to have to establish down in engineering."

"How long?"

"Our diagnostic test is almost done. We've identified the weapon station and we *think* they might just be off. AI is running a test too."

"Sounds good. Keep the line open."

Olly worked with Cathleen to get the database working. The reboot gave them access to another node but it was merely a junction, a launching point for other information centers throughout the network. She identified a link which they could use to bring someone out of the suspended animation process, resuscitating one of the crew.

Together, they ran a scan to identify the various personnel in an attempt to locate someone suited to computer systems. If they followed any best practices concerning security, only a few people would have the necessary access codes to get Protocol Seven. Whoever they revived first needed to help immediately or it may be pointless to wake anyone else.

Maria spoke up on the com, "Engineering wasn't as prepared as the bridge but I've got all the consoles running. The universal code helped my tablet gain access and is translating all the protocols. Weapon systems are definitely offline but I'm rerouting power and am replacing some burned out parts."

"ETA?" Olly asked.

"A couple minutes," she replied, "however, I don't know how long they'll last under a prolonged engagement. Hell, I don't even know what their weapons will do. Are they going to be powerful enough to get through the enemy's shields? No clue."

"Speaking of defenses," Olly added, "can we power them up?"

"You said weapons were priority number one," Maria said. "I can look at them when I'm done…"

"Multitask," Olly answered. "We have to be efficient."

Maria sighed. "Yes, sir. I'll do what I can."

"Lieutenant Darnell," Sid piped in, "the Behemoth is under attack."

"What?" Olly tapped into the Silver Star cameras to see what was going on. The enemy ships bombarded the Behemoth, bringing down a lot of firepower on them. "Holy crap! Guys, we really need to hurry! Our people are being hit hard!"

"What?" Maria shouted. "What do you mean?"

"The enemy's all over them!" Olly paused. "Fighters are engaged…wait…the enemy ships were on their way to *us*! AI, why would they attack this ship?"

"This vessel has been pursued by the enemy for some time," Sid replied. "Protocol Seven has required their full attention to take us down at all costs."

Olly groaned. "Why didn't you say so before?"

"No one directed such a query to me before."

"Thanks for nothing." Olly shook his head. "Lisa, Maria, they're after *us*! The Behemoth is just in the way. You're working toward self preservation with our offensive/defensive capabilities."

Agatha pinged him and he brought the bridge online. "Darnell here."

"Olly, it's Captain Atwell. We're in a serious way here and need some help. Tell me you got those weapons online."

"We're working on it, sir. Maria's almost got them."

Gray sighed. "I don't have to tell you this isn't a request. You guys need to be able to hit them or we're all dead."

"I know, sir...there's only so fast we can go with repairs though."

"Sir!" Maria interrupted. "I got the primary power conduit restored and shoved a new fuse into the console. A compensator went out but they're modular so I replaced it like a battery. The rest of the machine—"

"Are they up or not?" Olly interrupted.

"We're good! Weapons are charging now! Holy wow, it's fast! We'll be ready in ten seconds!"

"Did you hear that, Captain? We're weapons hot!"

"Thank God," Gray replied. "You have someone ready to fire?"

"Lisa, please tell me you know how to pull the trigger."

"Sid showed me," Lisa said. "We're good."

"On your command, sir! I'm tapping your com into Lisa's. We're ready when you are."

***

Gray let out a deep breath and stood from his seat. "Okay, Lieutenant Oxton, lock your weapons on the nearest enemy. Redding, link up with her and coordinate your fire. I want you guys to give them everything we've got. Don't hold back. This literally is a matter of life and death."

"Understood." Redding acknowledge, tapping her controls. "I'm linked up with you, Oxton. On my mark, we'll turn and fire. Ready?"

"Ready!" Lisa replied, her voice taught with nerves. Gray hadn't heard someone so scared in a long time. Most of his bridge crew were cold as ice. The technicians weren't as akin to combat or so prepared for that matter. They weren't in this for the fight, they wanted to keep things running.

We all stretch when the need arises.

The Behemoth ponderously turned, straining the sluggish engines. Gray clenched his fist tightly, willing the vessel to move faster. Every fiber of his being tingled with adrenaline. If this worked, if their coordinated effort drove the enemy off, then they certainly took the upper hand. They could win the fight.

Otherwise...

He didn't allow himself to consider the alternative. This had to work. Too many lives were at stake for it not to.

"Enemy fired again!" Everly leaned forward, reading his tablet. The ship jostled. "Direct hit! Lower decks!"

"Redding!" Gray spoke her name through clenched teeth.

"We're in position now, sir." Redding looked up at the screen then squinted at her console. "Okay, Oxton...on my mark. Three..."

Gray stood up, watching the screen through squinting eyes. The enemy floated out there, maintaining their distance and formation. They only moved to aim, spinning in place and not pulling away from their position. This gave the Behemoth a slight advantage in distance and the ability to make minor adjustments to avoid extra damage. Sadly, it didn't seem to be working.

"Two..."

Gray noticed the enemy weapons were charging again, the barrels of their pulse cannons glowing in anticipation. Their entire engagement would be decided in the next few seconds. How did the enemy recharge so quickly? Their fusion cores must be huge, and possibly not as contained. Safety conditions on their vessels may not be a concern.

"One..."

The enemy would fire any second! Gray looked at his tablet to see why they delayed at all and understood at once. Redding used the extra few seconds to better line up their shot, to get a solid lock. As he said before, he wanted certainty of a direct hit. Her last few seconds were well spent but they'd be for nothing if they didn't fire first.

"Fire!" Redding shouted, jabbing her console several times.

The Silver Star's edge lit up, not one but *hundreds* of tiny barrels all launching pulse energy in a massive, concentrated blast. Combined with the Behemoth's attack, all of space turned white for a brief moment. The shielded enemy ship took the brunt of the attack, canceling their own attack and causing massive damage. The other caught some secondary blasts and careened away, moving off from its companion.

"Direct hits!" Redding shouted.

"Damage readings coming in now," Paul said. "Wow, they really took a pounding! I'm reading fires on their decks but a hull breach will have them out shortly. At least two weapon systems are offline or at least, I'm not reading any power from those stations."

"Are they going to stick around?" Everly said. "Or do they want to keep going toe to toe?"

Redding spoke up, "Oxton reports she'll be able to fire again in a few moments."

"Get ready for another volley," Gray said.

"They seem to be pulling away!" Tim announced. "They're moving out of range!"

Gray sat in his chair, allowing himself to relax for a moment. His reprieve was short lived and he leaned forward to assess the situation. They sustained some pretty serious damage and it impaired combat effectiveness, at least for the moment. The battle moved them toward a real stalemate. Neither side could afford another exchange so they each retreated, licking their wounds while hunting for another advantage.

"Olly, get your shields back up as soon as possible," Gray said, then clicked over to Chief Engineer Higgins. "You've got limited time. What can you do with it?"

"What's limited?" Higgins asked. "Because an hour is a lot different than fifteen minutes."

"I can't say for sure. Let's go in half hour increments."

"In a half hour, I can contain the worst of our damage and get auxiliary power to the engines. Weapons are mostly stable…I'll put someone on ensuring consistent energy flow." Higgins sighed. "I'll do what I can. Let me know if I have more time."

"Do what you can." Gray turned to Everly. "I want the current fighters onboard and launch the others to replace them. Keep us battle ready. Can the hangars handle the traffic?"

"Yes, sir. Control's ready to go and will bring them in and out as necessary."

"Keep a steady escort until further notice." Gray took a moment to consider the situation. The Silver Star came through for them and they survived the assault but the next step involved getting Protocol Seven. He hoped it didn't turn out to be a wild goose chase, some fringe theory of a dead culture. They put a lot of faith in these visitors to provide a solution.

He reviewed the battle on his tablet and something interesting caught his eye. The enemy fighters did not attack the Behemoth. They went after the Silver Star. Made a straight line for it in fact. Why? The ship's weapons were down and posed no threat. Maybe they didn't come to Earth for an attack on humanity. Maybe they wanted to take down the Silver Star…

This gave some credence to the voracity of this Protocol Seven, sure. The enemy clearly worried about it. *Now we need it more than ever.* Gray leaned back and considered their positions, just out of weapons range.

Were his opponents worrying about what his people would discover enough to push them into a mistake? He sure hoped so. If Protocol Seven proved to be as valuable as it seemed, it might well turn the tide of the war.

I can't get ahead of myself. One battle at a time. The overall conflict, the Alliance's multi front war zone, couldn't be his concern at the moment. All his focus remained on staying alive and defeating this incursion. When they wrapped them up, they might have plenty of time to worry about galactic affairs. Right now, Earth required all their attention.

Remember, we're the shield...not the arrow. Not yet at least.

They had two dangerous adversaries repairing as much damage as they could before another assault. Gray devoted all his attention to them and what they represented. Events already played out differently than the previous visit by these bastards. The Behemoth stood prepared for a real engagement and didn't fold at the first sign of trouble.

That alone provided the Captain with confidence. They could hurt their opponents and more importantly, had the ability to win. Their tactics proved sound. If the Behemoth carried them the final mile, they'd very well make history and if they didn't...well, history might not matter to anyone anymore.

It's all a matter of perspective. As Redding said, no pressure....

Chapter 14

Tech crews worked feverishly on the Silver Star. Olly focused on the suspended animation chambers. Reliable power was restored but the program to revive the occupants would not successfully execute without errors. This meant Olly had to work with Sid to debug the code and recompile it. They'd already made three goes at it with a fourth underway.

Cathleen continued to tinker with the database but struggled with minor corruption. She isolated bad entries and used the universal code to clean it up. Every step required painstaking focus. One mistake set her back to the beginning and she made incremental backups to ensure her work wasn't lost.

The engineering bay proved to be in much better condition than anticipated. After rebooting systems, Maria was able to support the efforts of the other technicians. She routed power, provided access to computing power and established solid connections with the bridge. When she finished her work, the Silver Star would be ready for manual operation again.

This meant the consoles on the bridge were all active. Lisa went beyond the weapons to scans, navigation and piloting. She had the screen working and cameras hidden all over the hull provided high resolution, real time images of space around them. The Behemoth established a connection with their computer and synched up their maneuvers, allowing them to adjust formation.

"I've analyzed the enemy tactic," Cathleen announced, making Olly jump. "Sorry, sir. I've found a cache of scans from when they attacked these people. It's brief, but they didn't detect them until they started firing."

"What did they learn?" Olly asked.

"It's some kind of sensor blindness," Cathleen replied. "A low level radiation blast that confuses scans. That's why our people thought they disappeared."

"Why'd they suddenly reappear? How'd our scans pick them back up?"

"It's not a constant pulse," Cathleen continued. "From what these people discovered, they've got roughly a minute of stealth."

"Send it over to me," Olly squinted. "Maybe I can come up with a counter."

"Aye sir."

Olly frowned as the information filled his screen. The radiation had to be low enough to not be noticed but a specific potency to impede sensor equipment. Compensating for it, now that they knew, wouldn't be too difficult. A quick recalibration would do the trick and if they had the process queued up, they'd be back in business in *seconds.*

Plenty of time to counter an attack.

He wrote up the program and sent it over to Paul with a note on how it worked. Lisa received it next with a request to plug it into the consoles on the bridge. *Glad to take your little advantage away. What've you got next, you bunch of bastards? Believe me, we'll counter that too*.

Olly returned to his attention to the suspended animation pods. These guys liked to posture and show their muscles but they were learning humanity wouldn't just roll over for them and die. It was a lesson Olly hoped would be particularly painful.

***

Gray read over the discovery of how they didn't see the enemy attack them. He shared it with Clea and shook his head. A simple trick, hardly rocket science, blew out their sensors and blinded them. In another time, before their upgrades, they would've died. But they didn't and now, his people learned to counter their nonsense.

If only we would've been one step ahead instead of three steps behind that time. He'd been so proud of himself with the bomb trick, this bit of humble pie tasted all the more foul. He deserved the self chastisement but didn't have the time. He shook it off and directed his attention forward.

The enemy maintained their distance, probably still conducting repairs. A half hour stretched to an hour. Higgins reported more systems restored. Eventually, one side or another had to crack and attack again. The trick involved risk analysis. Were they combat effective enough to survive a second engagement? More importantly, could they catch the enemy unprepared for the next bout?

"Sir?" Agatha broke through his concentration. "We're being hailed."

"The enemy?" Gray exchanged a glance with Everly.

"No, they're channel states they're with the African League. It's the ADF Nile."

"Paul? Do you have them on scan?"

"Aye." Paul checked something on his console before continuing. "They're on a rapid approach from the enemy's flank."

"What the hell are they doing?" Redding asked. "They're not planning on joining the fight, are they?"

"If they do," Clea said, "they'll be slaughtered."

"Play their message, Ensign," Gray said. "Let's see what they have to say."

A voice crackled over the speakers immediately. "This is Captain Jaren of the ADF Nile. We are here to engage the enemy and lend the Behemoth any aid it may require. Our superior firepower and technology will make us more than a match for the invading force."

Clea's brows shot up. "I believe they are actually insane."

"Any truth to what they're saying, Paul?"

Paul shook his head. "Conventional weapons, sir. They don't even have a pulse drive to speak of. Maneuverability is hampered by old thrust engines...their core is fusion...its state of the art for what it is but if they start trouble with the enemy ships, they won't stand a chance."

Gray engaged the communicator. "Captain Jaren, this is Captain Atwell of the Behemoth. Withdraw from the combat zone immediately. You do *not* have the firepower to deal with this threat. The enemy we're facing has superior armament and defenses. Your weapons won't even penetrate their shields. I repeat, withdraw immediately!"

"You have nothing to worry about with us, Captain Atwell," Jaren replied. "We are well trained and prepared for this engagement. We appreciate your concern but it is unnecessary."

Gray slapped his arm rest. "Don't be a fool, Jaren! I'm not telling you this because we're too proud to accept help! We don't want your people to die in a pointless exercise of vanity!"

"They've cut the transmission, sir," Ensign White said.

"They're advancing!" Tim shouted. "Look! They're actually moving in to engage!"

"God damn it!" Atwell gestured at Redding. "Turn us around, they're pushing our hand. Get in there to help! White, radio the Silver Star and tell them to engage immediately. All pilots, hit them *now*! Make it happen, people! The Nile doesn't stand a chance without us."

Everyone on the bridge sprung to action. Everly hit the coms with Revente, White contacted Olly and the ship began to move, fully powered and ready for action. The enemy powered up their own weapons as the Nile closed within range. The Behemoth shoved ahead, closing distance.

"I don't think we can make it in time, sir," Redding said. "I'm pushing it and we've got one hundred percent power but this...this doesn't look like we can make it."

"Don't say that," Gray replied. "Just concentrate."

And pray the Nile can survive long enough not to get blown straight to hell.

"Thirty seconds to range," Paul announced.

"Twenty," Tim corrected. "Thirty for the Silver Star."

Gray turned to his tablet and cursed under his breath. The Nile would be on the enemy in ten seconds and was probably already in range of their weapons. Pulse blasts erupted from the invading forces, cutting into the Nile and blowing straight past their inferior shields. Everly stood and took two steps forward, staring at the screen with wide eyes.

"Push it, Redding!" Gray grunted through gritted teeth. "They don't have a lot of time!"

The Nile fired a volley of missiles, each one ineffectually flashing against the shields of the enemy as if they were no more than space pebbles crossing the wrong path. A second barrage of pulse lasers struck the Earth ship, this time causing catastrophic damage. Gray watched helplessly as the ship parted in the center, bubble explosions occurring along the hull before the engines caught.

Agatha stiffened seconds before the entire ship went up, pieces of the wreckage flung off into space. "I...I heard them scream..."

Everly turned to her. "What was that?"

"Their coms were linked to mine..." She trembled. "I heard them. Just before the explosion...I heard them."

"Slow down," Gray muttered. "Cancel the attack order. Pull back to our previous position."

"Sir?" Everly turned on him, scowling. "They just annihilated an Earth vessel! Murdered every single person on board!"

"I'm aware of that, Adam." Gray returned his severe look. "But blindly rushing in and attacking at this moment wouldn't exactly do us any favors. We have a plan...find out what the Protocol Seven is. When we have it, we'll employ it and send those dogs straight back to whatever hell they crawled out of.

"In the meantime, we will fight this battle with patience, strategy and intelligence. A full on assault right now, even with both ships, is not a guaranteed victory."

"My experience suggests attacking at a time like this is the unexpected thing to do," Everly replied. "We go in and get them after they've had a quick victory...and show them what it means to mess with us."

"But yours isn't the experience we're listening to today," Gray said. "Kindly work with Paul to see if there are any survivors from that explosion...escape pods or shuttle craft. Our first order of business is to save lives. Not risk our own seeking vengeance."

"Yes, sir." Everly sat down, albeit in a seemingly grudging manner and spoke quietly with Paul.

Gray remembered the first engagement with the enemy. He saw people die then too and it affected him just as much now as then. These people, the soldiers who attempted to help, only meant to protect their planet. Not wise, but their hearts and souls were in the right place. Like every other being, they only wanted to keep those they loved safe.

Whatever vanity or arrogance pressed them on cost them their lives but these invaders, these warmongering aliens were to blame. If they hadn't gone on a galactic wide rampage, countless dead would still be alive. On all sides of the conflict, enemy, Alliance and human. No wonder so many banded together to stop them.

As Gray looked over the people on the bridge, he recognized the same grim determination in their expressions as he felt in his soul. He never doubted anyone's determination but even the coolest individual must've felt some heat in their blood. Witnessing the death of so many human beings elevated their resolve.

"It's the right decision," Clea said.

"I don't need you to tell me that."

Clea shrugged. "I was under the impression that humans appreciated validation from time to time."

"Now's not that time." Gray turned to her, softening his severe expression. "I'm sorry. But in this case, after what I just saw…I want to do what Adam suggested but I know it's the wrong course of action."

"Yes, we both know impulsive behavior costs lives." Clea turned to the view screen. "And our enemies seem to have a knack for taking advantage of weaknesses."

"I can't wait to exploit theirs." Gray hit his com, connecting with Engineering. "Higgins, you'd better have some good news for me. You've got another few minutes for repairs. How much do you have left to do?"

"The hull damage has to wait until we can safely dock," Higgins replied, "but those decks are sealed. All systems have been restored. I've had to do some rerouting of power and such but weapons, shields and engines are all ready to go."

"Fantastic. Let's hope the Silver Star has as good of news."

I sure could use a little right about now.

Chapter 15

Lines of code flew across Olly's screen, the twenty-third attempt to run the revival program without errors. It ran through each command, checking them for errors and corruption. The whole process took less than a minute but each second felt like eternity. He willed it to go faster, wishing for an instantaneous option.

The environmental suit was becoming beyond uncomfortable. Yes, the atmosphere in the ship stated it would sustain human life but none of them wanted to trust it. They remained safe in their protective gear so no one had to worry about a sudden change in temperature, oxygen or even compression.

I can't wait to get back aboard the Behemoth.

From what Olly could tell, Paul did a fine job filling in for him. As the fourth shift guy, he proved himself big time. Would Olly have caught the radiation burst weapon? Probably not but the question would be asked in a postmortem analysis of the situation. Every decision, every action needed to be examined, justified and explained.

Unfortunately, the spirit of improving processes felt an awful lot like persecution but most of it would fall on Captain Atwell and Commander Everly. They always seemed prepared for such trials and knew how to play the games. Maybe they took a class he didn't know about in the academy, something specific for command structure.

Bureaucracy 107, how to survive a full evaluation after a major engagement or mission. Even his made up class sounded boring as all get out.

Olly's heart raced when the it finally finished, pausing for validation. He tapped his leg and bobbed his head, impatient for the results. Would he have to start again? He allowed a little hope to drift into his heart but deep down, he figured it would fail. A pessimistic side of him suggested the system was too far gone to fix and that he wasted his time.

Don't give into that crap, Darnell! You've got this!

He stiffened when the final line came back green...the code recompiled successfully. It ran without an error. *Success?* He double checked the final log file and nearly whooped like the marines had earlier *Dear God...it* is *a success!*

"Guys! I did it!" Olly called into his com. "I got the revival program operational!"

"Are you kidding?" Cathleen joined him. "I can't even believe it. That code was seriously hosed."

"I know, right?" Olly shook his head. "Do we have access to the personnel database?"

"Let me look..." Cathleen paused to look over her own findings. She cleaned up a lot of data without even looking at the results. Now, she went back through and sent a link to Olly's tablet. "It looks like we're in luck. Personnel, specialty *and*, the part you need...pod number."

"Fantastic!" Olly got the list of names and started scanning their specialties. Most of them were not military. Artisans, corporate workers, home makers, some children...normal citizens. The people meant to crew the Silver Star came up toward the end. Five naval soldiers and before them, a dozen ground troops. He picked the highest ranking officer. "How about this guy?"

Sid translated his title to *Captain*.

Cathleen nodded. "Yeah, he'd have access to all systems, right?"

"You are correct, Ensign Brooks. Captain Andu Paltein does have full security rights to the ship."

"Can he give us Protocol Seven?" Olly asked.

"Affirmative. He does have access to such sensitive data."

"Okay, I'm going to start the revival process." Olly turned to the marines. "Be on the lookout for activity from one of the pods! I'm waking someone up who can help us!"

The soldiers went on high alert but Olly ignored them, going back to the application. It took several moments for it to initiate the process but once it did, they started to hear it in action. First, a hissing sound from a pod near the center of the room. The globe behind it throbbed, growing brighter before dimming. It repeated the behavior over and over as Olly's console gave him a status update.

The person's heart rate climbed and their vital organs essentially woke up. Respiration returned to normal levels and the body temperature rose to only slightly higher than a human. Before five minutes ran out, Captain Paltein entered regular sleep state. The suspended animation ended.

"How do we open the pod?" Cathleen asked. Just as she finished, the top melted away into the body, revealing a humanoid male with blue-black hair, smooth, slightly golden skin and several days of beard. He wore a skintight, blue suit that covered his feet but left his hands free.

The others gathered around him with Olly standing in the back. Marines held their guns at the ready, seemingly prepared for an attack. They waited quietly until the Captain gasped and arched his back. At first it looked as though he were in pain but they quickly realized he was simply stretching.

"Captain Paltein?" Olly asked. "Can you hear me?"

Sid translated automatically, issuing a series of odd syllables that made Olly's tongue ache just thinking about trying to speak them. The man blinked, peering up at them through bright, teal eyes. They widened and he struggled to move but hadn't fully recovered yet. He settled into the chamber, terrified but unable to leave.

Olly held up his hands. "We're here to help..." *Damn, the helmet!* He really didn't want to take it off but it might be the only way to get the guy to calm down. He disengaged the safety locks and twisted it to the right before pulling it off. "See? I'm a human...humanoid...like you. We just want to help. Your ship found the friendly culture it was looking for."

Sid continued speaking, giving the Captain the words as quickly as Olly spoke them. It did not visibly sooth Captain Paltein but he did reply in his language, mostly mumbling a response. When he finished, Sid paused a moment before translating.

"He says he doesn't know what you're talking about and asks how he got here. He also wonders if you have kidnapped him."

Olly sighed. "Sid, please let him know that we've woken him up from the suspended animation pod. Tell him we're here to help."

Cathleen tapped him on the shoulder. "The physical trauma of the suspended animation has affected his brain. I did a scan. I'm not medical track, but the tablet states he's suffering from a form of amnesia. Must be a side effect of the process."

"No!" Olly shook his head. "The program *worked*! I got it fixed. This…this shouldn't have happened."

"It is not the programs fault," Sid stated. "This suspended animation technique was untested. Our people only just perfected it to not kill the inhabitant of the pod."

"What do we do?" Cathleen asked. "I don't think we're equipped to help him."

Olly stepped away, head bowed in thought. The Silver Star must've had a medical bay but then, they might've been standing in it. He could wake up a doctor but if they experienced a side effect as well, they'd have two people to care for instead of one. No, they needed a doctor to take care of this. None of his tecks could do anything for the captain.

"We have to get him back to the Behemoth." Olly stepped over to the console. "Sid, can you download to a device? Something so Captain Paltein has a translator?"

"Affirmative. Please see the shelf to your right."

Olly turned just in time to see a part of the ship melt away, revealing small, flat devices neatly lined up. He pulled one out. "Is this a tablet of some kind?"

"A mobile processing device. Your people call them computers and tablets. Simply place it near the console and I will transfer a copy of myself to the device."

"It's not network capable, is it?" Cathleen warned. "I like Sid and all, but I think people would go nuts if he copied himself over to the Behemoth computers."

"I will not ingratiate myself on your computer devices, Ensign Brooks. You have nothing to worry about."

Olly did as he asked and shrugged at Cathleen. "Not that we have a lot of choices here. We can't speak to the guy and if he ends up on our ship, he has to talk, you know? Besides, I trust Sid. He hasn't screwed us over yet and I don't see why he would now. We're saving these people after all."

Cathleen held up her hands. "You don't have to convince me."

Olly tapped his com and brought up Captain Hoffner. "Sir, we have revived one of the crew but he requires medical attention. I'd like to get him to the Behemoth as soon as possible."

"What's wrong with him?" Hoffner asked.

"Amnesia brought on by untested suspended animation," Olly replied. "Plus, we're pretty sure he needs to be checked over. This was experimental for them and God knows what else it did to him."

"I trust he doesn't speak English like the AI?"

"No, but we have a translation device he can take with him which will allow our staff to communicate with him."

"Escort him to the hangar," Hoffner replied. "I'll get the Behemoth to send over a medical shuttle ASAP."

"Sounds good." Olly turned to Captain Paltein. "Sir, we need to get you to the medical bay."

Sid's translation seemed to make the man nervous but he agreed in his language.

"I don't think he should walk," Olly said. "Do you have a gurney or anything here, Sid?"

"Affirmative. Please check in the back of the room. I have opened the storage room where some medical supplies are stored. Sadly, the perishables have lost their seal and are no longer good but the gurney will be quite sufficient to transport Captain Paltein to your vessel."

"Cathleen, grab a gurney while I tell the Behemoth what's going on." Olly stepped away and let out a deep breath. "I'm pretty sure they're going to have a thing or two to say about this."

***

Everly tapped Gray's arm. "Captain, I've got Olly on the line. He says they've woken up the Captain of the Silver Star. Apparently, he's suffering from side effects of suspended animation. Hoffner just requested a medical shuttle. They'd like to bring this person to our sick bay."

Gray nodded once. "Make it happen."

Clea stood. "I'd like to meet them in the hangar if you don't mind."

"Think you can help?" Gray asked.

"Most definitely. An alien being who likely does not speak our language might feel a little better if someone else stands out with him."

"Good thought." Gray gestured for the door. "Let us know what you find out right away."

"Sir," Paul spoke up as Clea left the room. "Getting a shuttle over here won't exactly be easy. I mean, we've got full shields up, not to mention the enemy close enough to spit at."

Redding huffed. "If they were that close, I'd be blasting the hell out of them."

Paul rolled his eyes. "You know what I mean. We start sending shuttles around, we're asking for trouble."

"The decision's been made, Paul," Gray replied. "Focus on your duties. Everly, give the shuttle a fighter escort. I'm sure they won't need it but better to be safe than sorry."

"On it."

"Okay, let's see what this guy has to offer." Gray settled back in his chair and watched the view screen. *This could be the break we've been waiting for or a total red herring. Let's hope fate feels generous. She's been pretty fickle most of the day.*

***

Captain Paltein clung to his translation device as if his life depended on it. He rode the gurney staring straight up with wide, frightened eyes. Two marines walked him down to the hangar with Olly in tow. The latter spoke to him the whole way, offering as much comfort as he could muster.

When they arrived, Olly asked Sid to open the hangar bay doors. The green of the shield lit up the room and they saw fighters flying around outside, patrolling the area. Far off, beyond their vision to the left, the enemy gathered waiting for their opportunity to strike. Whatever damage their ships sustained seemed to be enough to keep them away.

Just stay away a little longer, Olly's hopeful thought made his body tense. *This guy's been through enough without you stampeding in to give him a heart attack*.

***

Lieutenant Richard Martin and Lieutenant Kelly Parson drew escort duty for a medical shuttle. Panthers Seven and Eight respectively, they were the newest members of the team, which was likely why they got the crap duty. They sidled up to the hangar, waiting for their charge to deploy for the quick trip over to the Silver Star.

"Hey, Kel," Richard said, "you ever think we'd be in an actual fight like this?"

"Yeah," Kelly replied. "I knew the enemy would be back."

"I didn't. I figured why bother? We kicked their asses before. Why come back?"

"No one went and told the bad guys we won, you realize that, right?"

Richard paused. "I…didn't think about that. But shouldn't it be all the scarier? When your people don't return, wouldn't you assume the worst? We sure did with our probes beyond the Solar System."

"We always intended to follow up though."

"True that." Richard checked his scans. The enemy seemed to be holding their ground. "I guess they don't want any more today."

"They'll be back in," Kelly replied. "Revente's briefing proves it. Whatever damage we inflicted might already be repaired. The final fight's going to be rough and I promise you this, it'll start suddenly."

"You're all sunshine and rainbows, Kel." Richard shook his head. "A real motivator."

"I just like to keep it real, pal." Kelly went silent for a moment. "They're launching the shuttle."

A moment later, the medical craft left the Behemoth and gunned the throttle, heading for the Silver Star. Kelly and Richard took up flanking positions slightly behind it, following at a reasonable distance. They established a communication link and Richard gave them some brief instructions.

"Don't get too far ahead. We're not going to land with you but when you're ready to take off, let us know. We'll watch your six."

"Appreciate the protection, Panthers Seven and Eight. Glad to have you around."

"We're here for you," Kelly replied. "Just stay focused."

Richard watched his sensors like a hawk, waiting for an attack he hoped would never come. Hardly twenty seconds away, many other Behemoth fighters patrolled the area. If they got into real trouble, reinforcements were a quick jaunt away. Meagan made it clear the bad guys wanted the Silver Star for some reason. It dawned on him a medical shuttle carrying a survivor might just be a target too ripe not to pick.

The trip between ships took less than three minutes. The medical shuttle disappeared into the hangar, leaving Richard and Kelly to circle around and prepare for the trip back. Loading the patient shouldn't take too long. No more than five minutes he figured but probably less. Then they'd start back and the short but stressful escort duty would be over.

Then back to patrol.

"Panther Seven and Eight, this is Med One. We are securing the patient for transport. Estimated departure time, twenty seconds."

Even faster than I thought. Fantastic. Come on! Let's go!

"Hey," Kelly broke his thoughts. "I'm picking up some readings heading in fast."

"What do you mean?" Richard checked his scans. "I don't see…wait…there they are."

"Uh huh. Must be fighters."

"They're several minutes out," Richard replied. "Plenty of time to get this shuttle back if we hurry."

"Panther Five, this is Panther Eight," Kelly announced. "Can you bring Panther Six over here? We might have a problem."

"What's up?" Leslie Eddings, Panther Five, answered. "We're patrolling grid three-two-seven."

"Pretty sure they're more worried about getting this patient back to the Behemoth than the nothing you guys are finding in grid whatever," Kelly said. "Hurry up. We don't want to face down a bunch of fighters with this shuttle in tow. It's about to take off."

"Okay, okay," Leslie replied. "We're on our way."

Good call, Richard thought. *Still, it shouldn't matter. We'll have these guys home in no time.*

"This is Med One, launching now." The shuttle left the hangar and plunged toward the Behemoth at top speed. Richard and Kelly fell in beside it, easily catching up. Enemy fighters were closing in, picking up speed. Sensors estimated they'd overtake them *before* they reached the Behemoth.

"Crap." Richard sighed. "Do you see that, Kel?"

"Yeah," Kel acknowledged. "Leslie, prepare for a real fight. These jerks are almost on us after all."

"Fantastic. Do you have a number?"

"Not an accurate one," Kelly replied. "At least four…but probably more. They like to fly tight to avoid scan confirmation."

"This is Med One, we are raising our shields." This meant they'd be slowing down significantly. Holding off the fighters would not be sufficient. They'd have to take them out. A couple lucky shots would be all the enemy needed to destroy the shuttle. Protecting them would be a pain.

Richard sent a ping to Kelly, indicating he felt they should engage. She sent back an acknowledgement then let Panthers Five and Six know to catch up. Six committed to staying by Med One. Three fighters against whatever the enemy threw at them seemed like good odds. After all, they took down so many of them earlier.

"Visual!" Richard shouted. "Contact! Six total fighters."

"Great, and we're only bringing four..." Kelly sighed. "I hope you're ready for some crazy cause we've got it."

Richard pulled to the right and banked hard. Kelly went the opposite direction. They'd practiced the tactic a thousand times in simulation and training exercises. Earlier, they learned just how effective their unorthodox maneuver was against this particular enemy. Since they didn't seem to operate under the wingman mentality the humans trained for.

Coordination and cooperation went a long way and meant a lot more than numbers.

At least, Richard hoped so.

The enemy broke ranks, twisting away from their loose formation to meet the fighters. Others plunged straight for the shuttle, fully intent on annihilating it. "Um, Kelly do you see that?"

"Kind of busy right now," Kelly replied in a tight voice. "That's why we called in Five and Six."

Richard dodged a blast, dropped his ship under another to avoid a collision and buried the throttle. He pulled the trigger as he casually flew over one of the enemy and turned it into slag before initiating a barrel roll and joining back up with Kelly. His sensors suggested their first pass took out three fighters, leaving three others.

Five and Six engaged the attackers, driving them back from the shuttle. A random, lucky shot from the enemy tagged the shuttle, making the shield flash. Five dropped a missile which chased the fighter some distance before the fuel ran out and it exploded. Richard hailed med one.

"You guys okay?"

"Keep them off us!" The pilot yelled back. "We can't take another one."

As if it was our fault. Richard bit his tongue.

"Contact!" Kelly cried. "Six more!"

"Oh, hell with this." Richard lowered his head and plunged straight at one of the first three. The computer sought a lock while he dialed in to the open channel. "Mayday to any fighters in the area. We need additional backup ASAP. Over."

"This is Tiger Three," a voice answered. "We're en route to your position. Just hang on."

Solid tone sounded in his ears and he pulled the trigger. The shots hit the shields but didn't finish him off. The ship careened but maintained course and speed. Richard fired again, this time clipping the side of his target.

That did the trick and the ship spun out of control before exploding in a fiery globe.

"I got another one," Kelly said. "The last one's on his way to his buddies."

"This is Panther Six...I've been hit." Richard turned in his seat to try and see him. "I need to get back to the Behemoth. Stick is sluggish and shields are down."

"Get your ass out of here," Richard said. "You're not doing anyone good. We've got this. Look, Tiger Wing's here. We've got this."

Four Tiger wing ships joined them just as the enemy engaged. Richard had a last second to glance at his sensors to see that Med One was less than a minute away from docking with the Behemoth. They had to hold on for such a short period of time, just a little longer and the mission would be complete.

Now, with seven on seven, it seemed much more than possible.

Except that the enemy had a plan.

Two of the ships broke their formation and moved at full speed for Panther Six. "Stop them!" Kelly shouted, diverting her own ship to intercept. She was rewarded with a pulse blast that nearly took her out of the sky. Richard watched her spin away, only regaining control well out of the fight.

Panther Six attempted to evade but three solid hits tore his frame in half. The last thing Richard heard from his friend, Brian DuVall, was a short scream and half the word *eject*. A ball of gold flame burned out in an instant and then, the pilot and all traces he ever existed were simply gone.

The rest of the fight was a total frenzy of straight, concentrated violence. Panther and Tiger wing paired up, taking the enemy fighters down in rapid succession. Richard and his wingman, someone he didn't even bother to identify, closed on a target, dodging multiple pulse blasts before blowing their target to pieces.

Richard nudged his controls to the left, narrowly avoiding a shot straight to his nose. He played chicken with the other fighter, drawing him in. When they were within three hundred yards, he finally pulled the trigger, putting a round straight into what he assumed was the enemy's cockpit.

The shields flashed then the ship burst into flames, turning into little more than slag. Richard spun and dropped below the wreckage, entering the fray from the back. He counted only two enemies left but they didn't go down without a fight. Three ships from Tiger

Wing were destroyed though he saw their pilot beacons flashing for pick up.

Thank God, they got out.

One pilot was enough for the day.

"This is Med One, we have made it safely back to the Behemoth. Thank you for the assist, guys."

Yeah, whatever. "Let's mop these bastards up and go home."

Only the enemy ships bugged out and headed for home. "You still with me, Kelly?"

"Yeah, I'm here."

"I don't really feel like letting those pricks get away."

"Stand down, Panther Seven." Revente's voice came on the line. "Assist with pickup duty on the downed pilots. You'll have your shot at them again."

"Sir, they destroyed, they killed—"

"I know full well what happened," Revente interrupted. "Get back to the ship. That's a direct order."

Richard fumed as he thought about Brian, his whole body arguing against the command. Ultimately, he obeyed, even as he saw his friend's face in his mind's eye and desperately felt an urge for vengeance. More fighting wouldn't bring him back...but it just might make him feel better. The weight of the loss settled in as he turned his ship around and headed for home.

I sure hope that God damn shuttle was worth it. Richard drew a deep breath and let it out, trying to find his center. Sadly, that wouldn't happen any time soon.

Chapter 16

Chief Medical Officer Laura Brand had been busy. Her staff, spread out between two hospitals, handled a number of casualties from minor burns to far more severe lacerations. While the Behemoth seemed to come away from the skirmishes in reasonable shape, several of her crew bore the brunt of the damage.

The past hour and a half since the initial battle had her moving from table to table, double checking patients and the care plans of her subordinates. A vast majority of the hurt would survive and they'd only lost three patients so far. If she wasn't running around the room like a crazy person, she'd take a moment to knock on wood.

"Priority patient!" Someone shouted the words as they entered the room, pushing a gurney made of some kind of shimmering metal. Laura directed one of her nurses to take over stitching a young man's arm and rushed over to the pilots entering her hospital.

"What's going on? Who is this?"

"He's one of the crew from the alien vessel," one of the pilots explained. "Suffering from amnesia and complications resulting from suspended animation."

Laura's eyes widened. "Who sent you here with him? We don't know anything about his physiology let alone how to treat…complications."

"Orders from the Captain, Ma'am. We need to get back to our duties."

Laura watched the men leave, fighting back a feeling of exasperation. Turning to the person on the gurney, she admired his jet black hair and odd colored skin. Other than the cosmetic differences, he seemed to have all the parts of a human. Perhaps they could help him after all.

"Hello, sir, my name is Doctor Laura Brand. Do you understand English?"

He clung to a small device and it rattled something off in his language. He replied in a series of strange syllables, mostly mumbled. When he finished, the speaker on his device spoke up in a pleasant, articulate voice. "He does not speak your language, Doctor Brand. His name is Captain Andu Paltein."

Laura nodded. "Okay, Andu. I'm going to perform a diagnostic scan of your body and get a baseline. It won't hurt and you shouldn't notice anything at all but the device does make a sound. Try to remain calm."

The device once again translated. *Fascinating device. I wonder how it knows English*.

Idle curiosity had to wait. She drew out her tablet and initiated a diagnostic program, directing the hand held scanner over the alien's torso. Regular beeps emitted from the speakers as it collected data, analyzing his organs and brain waves. The process took less than two minutes and she drew away to check the results.

Body temperature: 99.2 degrees

If he had much in common with humans, he'd be running a little on the high side. *Possible side effect of waking up. The body might compensate for running cooler.*

Respiratory Rate: 26 BPM.

Also, slightly abnormal to humans. The average fell between twelve and twenty breaths per minute. *Could be nerves or another complication. We haven't done enough experimentation with suspended animation. This man is technically the first successful application of such a process.*

Heart Rate: 110 beats a minute.

A little fast, again, possibly from nerves. A foreign ship, new people, an uncertain future...Laura needed to learn whether fear motivated his various bodily functions or if this was normal for his people. They had no other examples to go by so Captain Paltein would be their baseline. Maybe if others woke up, they could develop some averages.

Organs were all in the right place for a human being and performed the same functions. His melanin levels seemed on par with humans but there was some other, unidentified chemical in his system causing the metallic sheen. Laura didn't feel comfortable giving him any drugs meant for humans but other, non-medical treatments, should be possible.

Laura tapped into Captain Atwell's line and paced away. "Hi Laura, what's going on?"

"I've got an alien in my hospital, that's what's going on," Laura replied. "What exactly did you think I could do with this man?"

"My report states he has some form of amnesia. Can you assist?"

Laura closed her eyes and shook her head. "With one of our own crew members? Probably, yes. But an alien? I mean, his body is quite a lot like ours but I have no idea what our drugs will do to him. I can't even speculate as to how he'd react to anything we throw his way. The best I've got is non-traditional practices, massage and…and acupuncture. Even then, I'll be guessing!"

"That's all I can ask for," Gray replied. "However, allow me to express the gravity of the situation: he has information that will allow us to possibly defeat the invading ships that entered our solar system."

"Great, no pressure, Gray!"

"I wouldn't have said that if it wasn't dire and he wouldn't be there if it wasn't important."

Laura sighed. "Understood. I'll do what I can. Brand out." She paced for a moment, head bowed in thought. The poor man must be terrified of what was happening and considering his situation, she didn't blame him. He woke up in the middle of a major battle amidst strangers, aliens without his memory.

We're lucky he hasn't lost his mind.

"Max," Laura called to one of the younger doctors. He was a slight man, no more than twenty-eight but a fantastic doctor. He graduated top of his class, the last one she taught. "We're going to need a full workup of our guest. Blood, tissue samples, the works *but* before we get into that, we have a pressing need to restore his memory."

"Doctor…" Max gave her a perplexed look. "I…do you know what you're asking? Amnesia can be caused by practically anything. Physical trauma, psychological…age. Any treatment we might offer depends on why he can't remember anything."

Realization struck his face. "You already know all of this."

"Yes, and in some cases, there's no treatment but giving the victim some time." Laura turned to the patient. "But we have to try something. We can't rely on any drugs, not without the workup to understand how they'd effect him. However, we can try some less evasive methods. Maybe some non-traditional concepts."

"Like what?" Max shrugged. "Massage?"

Laura smirked. "Funny, but not entirely out of the question. I'm going to do a thorough brain scan. Get the labs ready and let's hope he's not all that different from us."

"I'm on it, Ma'am." Max hurried off. Laura didn't disagree with his assessment. As was typical of high level command figures, they asked for results they didn't understand. *Just fix it* might work for an engine or computer but a living being didn't cooperate like technology. The biological machine analogy didn't hold true.

Laura joined Captain Paltein again, offering him a smile. "Sorry about the delay, sir. I'm going to do a thorough scan of your head, to see if we can do something about your memory loss. Again, it won't take long and it won't hurt."

The device translated and he replied. Again, the elegant voice spoke through the speaker. "He states that he is okay with you doing whatever you need to do but would like to better understand what is happening. What ship is he aboard and what has happened to his people?"

"Tell him he is aboard the USS Behemoth, a ship from Earth. His people are in suspended animation and just fine." Laura paused. "Also, let him know we're under attack by invaders and knowledge he possesses may save us all."

God, I hope that was the right thing to say.

When the computer finished translating for her, a look of determination crossed the man's face. He looked at her with his strange, teal eyes and smiled, albeit nervously. She reached out and gently touched his shoulder. The reassuring gesture had the effect she hoped for and he relaxed into the gurney.

Laura's scanner lit up as she held it near the crown of her patient's head. The tablet immediately displayed an image of his brain, a holographic representation that became more detailed the longer she held it there. The organ itself appeared to be the same as a human's and the activity appeared similar.

After a moment, the picture began to fill in with color. White parts were considered healthy with yellow points of concern and red outright damage. Luckily for him, nothing came back red but some yellow presented itself on the sides. She moved the scanner to the sides to collect more data including internal measurements of the skull.

Aha... Laura's back stiffened as she noted he was suffering from some minor swelling. *And therein lies the problem. I'm guessing the process of revival happened too quickly and caused some trauma to his organs. I'll bet when we do the complete workup, we'll find other, similar issues.*

"Max!" Laura called and he hurried over. "Brain swelling."

"What?" Max looked at the scans. "Oh my...subtle but...definitely enough to cause the symptoms."

Laura nodded. "Exactly. Now we just have to determine how we're going to reduce it safely. I have a thought. They have a tech crew over on the alien vessel."

"Yeah, I know Ensign Cathleen Brooks. Her parents were friends with mine. She mentioned she was heading over there."

"Can you reach out to them and see if they have access to any of their physiology records? We can at least determine if there are any allergies he might have as a species."

"I'm on it." Max stepped away and Laura returned to the Captain.

"Sir, we're going to take some samples of your blood and skin tissue. It's nothing to worry about. We just need to better understand your anatomy so we can help you. Okay?"

The computer translated then replied after the man muttered to it. "He says that will be fine, Ma'am."

"Okay, thank you. Here we go." *I hope Max finds something. We don't have time for a proper workup right now. Not with the way Atwell was talking at least.* She prepared a needle and offered him a thin smile. "Try not to look, sir. It hurts less if you don't see it coming."

***

Cathleen's com went off and she acknowledged it with a tap, still studying the console she worked on. "Ensign Brooks here."

"Hey, Cathy, it's Max. Do you have a quick second?"

"Only just. What's going on?"

"I've got the alien over here on one of my tables but in order to treat him, we need some more information. Organs and such seem to be in the right place but we have no idea if he's allergic to anything or if he might have special requirements that aren't being met. Do you have access to any medical records?"

"Checking." Cathleen tapped her screen. "Hey, Sid, do we have access to personnel records? Specifically, the medical kind?"

"Partially," Sid replied. "I will download them to your tablet."

"Max, I'm sending you what I've got. Don't know how complete it is…I'm cleaning up database corruption all over the place."

"If that's what you've got, it'll have to do for now," Max replied. "If you come across more, please send it over right away."

"Will do, Brooks out."

"Who was that?" Olly asked.

"One of the doctors. They needed medical records. How're you doing on your end?"

"I could wake them all up at this point," Olly said. "Looks like we've also got all shields, weapons and propulsion to one hundred percent. If we had a pilot up there, we'd be combat effective for sure."

"We sure gave it to the bad guys earlier."

"Yeah, I suspect that was because we surprised them." Olly joined her at her console. "Can you get us to a point where we can put in security clearance codes? If those doctors are successful, we'll need to enter that info fast."

"Sure, I've got a screen open in another task." Cathleen showed him. "Sid initiated it for me."

"Great." Olly patted her on the shoulder. "Hey, Sid, how long to open up all the databanks once we have some permission from your captain?"

"No more than one minute, sir. The data is available, but guarded. All but the fringe information Ensign Brooks has been working on is fairly well preserved. Storage managed the trip, and the various pitfalls, quite nicely."

"Sounds good. Let's keep on the ready. I have a feeling they'll get back to us soon."

I sure hope he's right, Cathleen thought, *for all our sakes.*

***

Max brought the information over to Laura, standing beside her with his tablet. "The medical records were translated by the ship's AI. They do not appear to be all that different from us. Stomach, kidneys, liver, all performing the same functions ours do. Furthermore, their blood composition is also the same."

"This lends evidence to the seed culture theory some scientists talk about," Laura said. "That some precursor race planted human beings on various planets."

"I wouldn't go so far as to call this proof of a fringe theory," Max replied, "but yes, it does elevate it somewhat. Before, it had barely any proof."

"Anyway, run a simulation and see what a shot of Neuron thirty-four would do." Laura hummed. "He's got a medium build so I'd say plug in twenty CCs. Should be sufficient to reduce the swelling and prevent any sort of blockage. The last thing we want is for him to experience a stroke."

"The simulation will take a good ten minutes or so."

Laura grinned. "You'd better get on it then. Time's a wasting."

"Yes, ma'am." Max headed off to his desk when the alarm went off. *What now?!* He thought. *Can we go thirty minutes without some disaster?*

"Imminent attack." Agatha White's voice blared through the overhead speakers. "All hands to battle stations."

Max sighed. *Apparently not.*

Chapter 17

Paul watched as their fighters screamed by to intercept the attacking force. This time, the enemy sent six fighters and a much larger ship with a sharp nose. He analyzed it's frame and signature but could not determine the purpose. It seemed like a shuttlecraft but bristled with weapons. He fed the info over to Olly but even he had no idea what they were facing.

"What're they doing?" Everly asked. "It looks like they're on a collision course!"

"Very possible," Clea replied. "Look at the design of that vessel."

Gray and Everly both squinted. "Oh my…" Gray muttered. "They mean to board us."

"That's my thought," Clea said. "I would lock turrets on and fire."

"Way ahead of you," Redding replied, tapping a button. Their weapons started firing, splashing off the shields of the shuttle as it barreled toward them.

"What the hell is powering that thing?" Everly shook his head. "How is it taking that kind of damage?"

Their fighters engaged, entering a wild dogfight with the other ships. A couple landed some decent shots on the shuttle but it continued pressing on, an unstoppable juggernaught ignoring all punishment they threw at it. It closed in with less than a thousand meters to go, Gray slammed his com.

"Security, prepare for intruders on Deck…" He checked his readings. "Thirty-two. They will be initiating hull breach in less than three minutes."

"What do they hope to accomplish?" Tim asked. "They can't possibly think they can *take* the ship! Not with the few guys they could fit on that thing."

"Maybe they don't have to," Clea replied. "Maybe they are here on a suicide mission."

"For what?" Redding asked.

"To kill our guest."

Realization hit Paul. It made perfect sense. If they worried the guy might impart the Protocol Seven information, then he had to die. He had the potential to turn the tide of the battle back their way and allow them to win. Such a concern might breed a desperate mission such as this but they had to know it was doomed to fail.

Or was it?

"Security, send a detail to the hospital." Everly must've read Paul's mind. He figured it would be a lot safer if they had someone guarding Captain Paltein rather than just praying they could hold them at the lower levels. Of course, that assumed the possibility the bad guys could get further into the ship.

Terrifying thought. Paul tried to focus on his scans, right up to the point he had to yell, "brace for impact!" a half second before the vessel struck them. It flew right through their shields and penetrated the hull, sliding neatly into the ship and wedging itself tightly in the hole. This allowed them to prevent the vacuum of space to suck them out when they disembarked.

God, I hope our guys are up for this! Paul watched helplessly as the security forces converged on the area. He took a moment to pray then leaned back and observed fate unfold in all its fickle glory.

***

Lieutenant Colonel Dupont coordinated his men, setting up check points in the event that the enemy broke through their lines. The area the invaders broke through gave them access to two different directions to take, constituting a two line front if they hoped to get further into the ship. Marines stationed in both corridors waited for the ship to open. They wore environmental suits in case the ship dislodged itself, leaving behind a hull breach.

His squads reported in that they were in position, six troops taking up both positions. Behind them, six more waited as reinforcements, there to prevent a deeper breach into the ship. Their orders were simple: kill the enemy at all costs. They carried heavy rifles and grenades to effect this command. Damage to the section was preferable to an escaped alien rampaging throughout the ship.

They broke through living quarters, destroying several of the rooms for the enlisted men. Luckily, everyone in that area happened to be on duty at the time and no one was killed. One man fell down who was halfway down the corridor and broke his wrist but otherwise, casualties were minor.

Dupont stood before his command screens, watching the helmet cams of his men as they aimed at the enemy ship. Tension remained thick as anticipation mounted. No one had seen the enemy face to face and the alliance didn't describe them either. This would be the first contact any of them had with the enemy in a combat situation. No longer separated by space and large vessels, they finally revealed themselves for what they were.

I doubt they're monsters. The thought made Dupont frown. Much as he wanted to believe the sentiment, a part of him didn't believe it. These bastards killed a lot of good men when they attacked before and he found out they did a lot worse to the alliance on several occasions. If they weren't beasts from horror stories, then he didn't know how he'd reconcile their atrocious actions.

Evil doesn't have to be ugly. Just ask Lucifer.

"Something's happening." The voice drew Dupont back to watch the screens. He saw the front of the vessel begin to open, revealing a black chamber beyond. When the panel stopped moving, it was easily wide enough to allow five or six men to pass through standing abreast. "No movement and motion scanners are negative."

"Don't rely on those," Dupont said. "We have no idea what these guys are capable of doing to our sensor equipment."

"Roger, sir."

The Behemoth corridors allowed for decent sized gear to travel anywhere in the ship. This meant three people could walk abreast comfortably. Dupont had his men practice combat maneuvers on every deck and they knew their way around better than anyone aboard. This also granted them the advantage of knowing how best to set up defensive positions.

When the first responders arrived in front of the enemy shuttle, they set down mobile cover, a large chunk of metal with handles roughly a meter and a half tall. Three men crouched in front of it, aiming their weapons over with three more behind them, prepared to pop up and fire as necessary. This was mirrored around the the corner.

Twenty feet behind them, other crews set up the same way. Guards were posted at the elevators and even the small access tunnels for maintenance. Dupont felt the area was as secure as it could be considering how the enemy penetrated their defenses. He doubted they had a similar tactic to get deeper into the ship.

And I'm pretty sure they're not immune to small arms fire.

Security forces carried cutting edge pulse rifles. Their rechargeable magazines fired a hundred rounds before needing to be replaced but after five minutes in a portable cradle, they'd be ready to go again. On Earth, they proved capable of cutting through titanium and the most powerful combat armor. Shipboard shields ignored them but an unprotected fighter would be in trouble if someone got a clean shot off.

"Contact!" Dupont leaned forward to see what one of his people saw. At first, he thought they issued a false alarm when four tall humanoids rushed from their shuttle. They wore black, bulky armor covering every part of their bodies. The helmets were all angles with two sharp points which seemed to make horns and a rounded space where a human chin might be. None of them seemed to be armed, or at least, their massive hands were empty.

The marines opened fire, their blasts splashing against the teal light of shields. Dupont couldn't believe his eyes.

They have personal shields?! Are you kidding me?

They'd toyed with the idea on Earth. The Alliance representative even offered some ideas and advice but they couldn't perfect it without burdening their soldiers under the weight of a bulky backpack. It worked for ground fortifications but people were out of the question. *I want that technology. We could change ground warfare!*

Providing we survive this encounter.

"Scatter your fire!" Dupont shouted. "There has to be a weak point! Spread it over the whole body!"

The first of the invaders reached his men's cover and casually grabbed the metal and threw it behind him. It clattered against the hull of their shuttle just as he threw himself on a marine. He lifted his massive fist to pummel the man but the other five soldiers dove in, dragging him off with all their effort.

Jesus Christ, I hope that's some kind of power assisted armor because if they're simply that strong… Dupont blocked the rest of the thought and glared at the screen. The marine who went down scrambled backward as one of his comrades placed his rifle directly against the face of the alien and pulled the trigger.

Despite all his struggling, he couldn't escape all those men holding him and when the gun discharged, it did so inside the shield. The body went limp and fell to the ground in a heap, taking three men with it.

On the other side, the other two tore through the blockade and slapped aside the marines before fleeing down the hall. "Breach!" A soldier's voice shouted over the line. "Heading down corridor seven and fast! Two contacts! Be advised, targets are shielded!"

The next group of men started asking questions but they didn't get any answers before the aliens were upon them. They unleashed a flurry of fire but once again, the attackers rushed, barreling through the marines like bowling balls. The scattered soldiers regained their feet and gave chase, calling ahead to warn the elevator defenders to watch their fire.

Back at the shuttle, the marines there approached the opening and cast lights within. There was nothing but an empty chamber, void of even seats. One small panel graced the smooth walls, presumably the button to open the door. Dupont shook his head, amazed by the way their enemy worked.

They had no intention of getting back to their people.

"Contact!" The elevator guards shouted.

"We're right on them!" Dupont watched the cameras as a full dozen marines sprinted down the hall as fast as they could. The elevator guards braced themselves. Their enemies finally slowed, perhaps knowing they couldn't burst through the doors of the elevator.

"They're cornered!" Dupont called. "This is when they become the most dangerous! Take them out, guys! Do it now!"

As predicted, the aliens went into a frenzy, flailing at anything close to them. One marine got tossed against a wall where he slumped to the floor, unmoving. Another took a backhand to the head and dropped like a sack of flour. The massive arms acted as battering rams and when one hit a wall, Dupont saw a dent.

It took three men to slow one down by jumping on its back. This hampered its ability to move enough for another to place his side arm against its chest and fire several shots. Each blow made it jerk unnaturally before it finally slumped under the weight of the soldiers who brought it to the ground.

A final shot to the head finished it off.

More marines converged on the scene, backing the final alien into a corner. It looked about frantically, seeming to search for any means of escape. Fifteen marines aimed their weapons at it, standing at no more than five feet away. It tensed up but before it could move, they all blasted away, concentrating their fire on the upper torso.

The thing's shields couldn't handle that much energy and after a brief moment of resistance, the shield vanished. No one stopped shooting and the body danced against the wall, thrashing its way to death with over a thousand rounds of ammunition to keep it company.

"Cease fire!" Dupont yelled. "It's done, guys! You got it!"

He had to repeat the order once more when an overzealous soldier put three more rounds in the thing's head as it fell to the ground.

"Okay, okay, let's secure the area, men. Stabilize the wounded and get them to sick bay right away." Dupont rubbed his eyes. "Report back in five minutes." He clicked over to the bridge. "Captain Atwell, the situation down here is under control. I've got some good news and bad news. Which do you want first?"

"I'd rather hear something positive."

"Okay, we've got some alien technology and bodies for research purposes. At least one of them is mostly intact. The shuttle's also undamaged."

"That is good. So what's the bad?"

"These things are bad news," Dupont said. "I'm sending you a video of what they're capable of. We're going to need to adjust our ground tactics to contend with that kind of threat…in a major way. I'm talking overhaul."

"Understood." Gray sighed. "Thank you, Marshall. Good job holding them back. We prevented them from whatever havoc they wanted to commit. I'd like to be present when you debrief your men."

"After we've won this battle, we'll all get together, Gray." Dupont smirked. "I kept up my side of things, now it's your turn."

"We're on it, my friend. We're on it."

Chapter 18

Gray finished watching the video of the alien attack and shook his head. These beings, whatever they were, lacked all self preservation. They fought zealously, heedless of repercussions or personal safety. Earth people dealt with such fanaticism before but this felt different. These...*things* for lack of a better word cared more about their cause than their lives.

The mission came first. It granted an insight into their enemy, a point which made them all the more dangerous. If they truly fell into a violent, quasi religious state, then humanity, and the alliance, needed to prepare themselves for some facts. First, there'd be no surrender without an extreme catalyst. Second, their people were willing to die so threats were useless.

Half measures left the table. They could only teach the enemy through total and complete victory.

Gray glanced at Clea. "Did you watch over my shoulder?"

"I did."

"Thoughts?"

Clea sighed. "They are pretty much as I always assumed they'd be. This assault, their actions in general, all prove they're little more than beasts driven by the will of another. Who designs their path, I don't know but when we find them, I can promise you they'll be the key to ending this war once and for all."

"I believe they attacked this way because they wanted to get at our visitor," Gray said. "And they figured three guys could do it."

"I completely agree. There's no other good reason for…well…for this."

A report came back stating all the marines survived but a few were in critical condition. One received a concussion and his doctor took him off active duty for two weeks. Another shattered his collarbone and would be in recovery for six weeks. The rest of the casualties involved sprains, bruises and some superficial cuts.

They'd all been very lucky.

Gray patched in to Laura. "Do you have anything for me yet?"

"We've *just* finished going over the biology we received from the alien vessel…er…the friendly one. We're about to risk an injection which should help him recover."

"How quickly, doctor?" Gray snapped. He closed his eyes and took a breath. "I don't mean to be testy but we're under the gun here."

"I understand. We're giving him a compound which is designed for extreme cases. In a small enough dose, it won't hurt him but it should reduce his symptoms enough to regain his memory. But Gray, I can't *promise* this will work. The man might simply need time. We don't know anything about suspended animation sickness."

"Let me know the moment he remembers something. Gray out." He stood and checked the scanners. The enemy remained where they were, holding their distance. Small skirmishes continued around them as fighters clashed but no real engagements occurred. The next one would be final. One side or the other had to lose.

It's all up to you who that is, Doc. Make this count.

***

"Doctor Brand?" Max hurried over to her. "The compound is ready. I've made some slight changes to account for his alien physiology. The info we got from Cathleen and our own tests indicated we needed to up the inhibitor in the drug to compensate for a rather high metabolism. His body will take to the shot *very* quickly."

"That's the first bit of good news I've heard," Laura replied, "but I know the risks that presents. If we give him too much, he might assimilate it all at once and simply die."

"Yes, the inhibitor will force his body to accept it at the interval we intend it to work. It's a slow release drug, meant to take several minutes. Even with my modification, I'm guessing we're going to see almost instantaneous results."

Laura nodded and extended her hand. "Give me the hypo. I'll administer it."

"Are you sure?" Max grinned. "You're not exactly the best when it comes to tapping a vein."

She widened her eyes. "Really? Who says?"

"Er…every patient unfortunate enough to have you poke them."

Laura shook her head. "Fine, you give it to him then, Mister Expert." She smiled. "See how you do on your next evaluation."

"I'm managing up, what can I say?" Max and Laura joined Captain Paltein on each side of his bed. He lifted his device so he could understand what they had to say. Max addressed him. "Hi, sir. We're ready to give you something which should help your memory. It's a shot though so it's going to hurt roughly as much as when we took a little blood, okay?"

A moment of translation passed before the device replied, "he states this is acceptable."

"Okay, here we go." Max pushed the man's sleeve up, revealing his wrist. He tensed his hand around the man's forearm, squeezing until the veins became prominent beneath the cool, shimmering skin. "I've got one." He pressed the needle down until he felt flesh surrender. A bead of blood appeared just as he depressed the plunger, administering the clear drug into the man's system.

"Now we wait."

The device translated then asked, "what're we waiting for?"

"Oh, that wasn't meant for him," Max replied, "but we just need to wait for the stuff to work."

"Understood."

Laura watched the chronometer on her tablet, counting along with the seconds. In a normal person, the compound would begin to take effect in five minutes. They gave him a quarter of the typical dose but even so, his body should accept it quickly. Visual confirmation may come in several ways from an expression to tension to a sudden recovery of his memories.

"Doctor," Max whispered. "Look."

Laura tore her eyes from the tablet, frowning at her patient. Captain Paltein tensed up, closing his eyes tightly. He writhed to the left, drawing his legs up toward his chest. Hands clenched then released and he opened his mouth as if to scream. *Did we screw up? Did he have an allergic reaction after all? Jesus, I have to get a scanner.*

Finally, he settled down, panting as if he just finished a marathon. His mouth opened slightly, jaw slack and eyes closed. Laura touched his arm, noting how cool his skin felt. She ran her scanner over him and the results shocked her. His temperature went down to what she'd consider human normal, his blood pressure and heart rate also slowed or, perhaps normalized.

Brain swelling can show through all manner of symptoms. Now that we know what their vitals should be, we'll have an easier time helping his people when we wake them up. Of course, it might be better to find one of their doctors before we do...

Captain Paltein opened his eyes as he caught his breath, stretching his neck. He pursed his lips and began rattling off information in his tongue, speaking so rapidly, Laura thought he might simply be making random sounds. *Perhaps I spoke too soon.* When he finished, the translation device spoke up.

"The Captain states he feels some minor discomfort but his memory seems to have returned. Exhaustion threatens to overwhelm him, however and he does not feel he has much time before he'll need rest. He has questions and possibly answers as well. First, he would like to know if his people are well."

Laura nodded. "They are still in the suspended animation chambers but all signs indicate they are fine."

The translator spoke to him. He mumbled back.

"Will you revive them as well?"

"Absolutely," Laura replied. "However, right now we need your help. We can answer all of your questions soon but right now, I believe we need something from you." She nodded to Max who tapped at his tablet.

"Cathy! This guy has his memory," Max's excitement came out in a boisterous lilt, a bit louder than was necessary and half a pitch higher than normal. "What do you need to know?"

"Olly!" Cathleen's voice blared over his speaker and he held it away. "The guy's awake and remembers stuff! What do we need?"

"Authorization for the databases," Olly shouted back. "His security code to get us in the computers and anything he knows about Protocol Seven!"

Max related the information to the captain and the device translated quickly. The captain sighed, his expression turning sad. "I understand," the translator declared for him. "I am sending his authorization codes to your tablet to transmit over to your crew. He states Protocol Seven was discovered at great personal risk to their intelligence agency. Through research and study, they found a structural weakness in the enemy shields, a flaw to exploit."

"I don't know anything about defensive architecture," Laura said, turning to Max. "Do you?"

Max shook his head. "Not a thing."

"I'm sure our people will make good use of this information," Laura patted the man on the shoulder. "Please, rest for now. We'll tell you everything else you need to know later…when things have calmed down."

The translator spoke again, "he states he appreciates all you've done and only wishes his people had encountered yours before the enemy. He believes your two cultures have much to share."

"I'm sure that's true." Laura smiled. "We'll talk soon, sir. C'mon, Max. We still have other patients to attend to."

***

Olly hurried to his console and entered the security codes from Captain Paltein. He stepped back and watched the screen intently, waiting for it to accept or deny his entry. Sid's strange, squiggly lines appeared and danced about, forming a multicolored wave form before finally settling on white.

A command line appeared but thousands of lines of code flashed by in a manner of seconds. He couldn't make any of them out but his tablet suggested the security protocols were lowering and, at the same time, rebuilding the database structures and links. Over the course of thirty seconds, he witnessed the computer essentially come back to life.

"Welcome to the Tam'Dral, Lieutenant Darnell," Sid's voice echoed through the room. "Now you know the true name of the ship you've been calling *The Silver Star.* You now have full access to all systems."

Olly and Cathy cheered, slapping each other on the backs but their excitement lasted only a moment. There was too much to do for celebration quite yet and they needed this Protocol Seven. He stepped forward and tapped away at the screen, searching the database for more information.

Exodus. An entry caught his eye and he sent it to his tablet before letting the system continue to search the archives for what he needed. As it started through the motions, he stepped back and turned on the video he downloaded. The description suggested Tam'Dral cameras recorded the footage.

The screen faded in to space with a brilliant, teal and green planet in the background. Three ships hovered in orbit bombarding the system. Bright, orange flashes appeared across the surface from pulse blasts and some other kind of attack he didn't recognize. They shrunk away just as the teal faded to a dull gray.

I just witnessed the death of a culture...and a whole lot more. Olly bit his lip and shook his head. *This could just as easily have been us three years ago.*

Cathy leaned on him while they watched and he offered her what comfort he could muster. Truthfully, he had a hard time not feeling a sick helplessness himself. The fighting nature of his people burned in his stomach and watching such injustice made him all the more passionate about stopping such atrocities.

"Protocol Seven located," Sid announced. "Downloading the information to your tablet right now."

"Thank you, Sid." Olly's excitement had been cowed by the video but his raw determination took over.

He read the information and stood up straighter. *This makes perfect sense.*

All shields operated through vibration frequencies, essentially, how fast they moved to stop incoming debris or weapons, depending on the grade. These were regulated through computer systems which randomized the speed so no one could match grade their settings and ignore them with a weapon.

Protocol Seven discovered the algorithm used by the enemy computers. By plugging this information into their scanners and matching them to their weapons, they'd anticipate the next cycle and blast straight through their defenses to the sensitive hull beneath. *This literally changes everything.*

And if the enemy didn't transmit back before they were destroyed, Protocol Seven would work in at least another engagement, if not more. The multifront war might be placated. The Alliance would have the upper hand. The galaxy itself might very well be rid of the enemy completely. *This* moment made the future a brighter thing.

Olly patched himself to the bridge of the Behemoth. "Captain Atwell, I've got some fantastic news."

"What is it, Olly?" Gray replied. "Do you have Protocol Seven?"

"Yes, sir," Olly confirmed. "I think it's time to share it with the enemy if you're so inclined. I suspect it's the type of surprise party we've been waiting to throw."

"Just tell us what to do and we'll bring the appetizers."

"It's on its way. I'll link up with Paul for the installation." Olly switched over to begin work, unable to stop from smiling. It lacked all mirth, more of a satisfying grin of potential victory. If it worked as advertised, they'd be on their way home soon. If not…well…one way or another, this battle was about to end.

Chapter 19

Clea read through the Protocol Seven information Olly sent and shook her head. *To think, this race we never encountered discovered a method of observing the enemy so well, they came away with such a weapon*. Their end saddened her. Such industrious, clever people should not have been beaten to the brink of extinction.

At least their spirit will live on and we'll certainly deliver their legacy to the enemy.

Clea's people definitely needed this information. She felt a sense of urgency building in her chest, a desire to communicate with them immediately. Unfortunately, even if such a thing were possible, they still had to win the fight. If any commander could see them through, it would be Gray. She knew him to be clever but after witnessing him through this engagement, she recognized he more than deserved the respect she paid him.

"Captain," Paul spoke up. "The enemy ships are on the move. They're closing in."

Everly scowled. "Maybe they think their little boarding party succeeded."

"Or maybe not," Gray replied. "They might be moving in to finish the job. I don't know if the invaders wanted to take care of the patient or cause havoc but they dramatically underestimated our people. They're about to make the same mistake again. Power up the shields and get us ready. Let's finish this once and for all."

"How soon before the Protocol Seven is ready?" Everly asked.

"Olly's got it installed on the Silver Star…er…Tam'Dral…whatever it's called." Paul paused. "We're at seventy-five percent on our end."

Gray frowned. "What's the delay?"

"The universal code had to translate it first. The algorithm itself is simple but interfacing it with our systems…that takes time."

"We don't have much," Clea said. "Will it be ready before they're within range?"

"I...think so."

Gray rubbed his forehead and sighed. "Fantastic. Hurry, Paul. That's not a request."

Clea moved over to Paul's station and looked over his shoulder. She scowled at the figures moving across. "Here," she pointed, "you can optimize this compiler. It's lagging."

"Oh, I see."

"Then, prioritize the network traffic there." Clea pointed. "That should enhance data flow and get this installed before we die."

Paul looked sheepish. "Thank you, Ma'am." He performed the tasks she suggested. "Captain, we're up to eighty-five percent."

"Does that mean you can give us an ETA?" Everly asked.

"Yes, sir." Paul paused. "Sixty seconds."

Gray stood. "Redding, range to targets?"

"Ten seconds for extreme range. Thirty for optimal."

"Maneuver us to engage. Have the Silver..." Gray frowned, "the Tam'Dral form up. Ensure we have a forward firing arc on both sides of their ships. I don't want them to do to us what we did to them. Position will be everything in this conflict."

"Don't like the real name?" Clea asked.

Gray shook his head. "It's not as romantic as mine."

"Fighters, sir?" Everly asked.

"Have all patrols come back aboard immediately." Gray checked the tablet and Clea leaned over to see. There were still fifteen ships combing the area. "Pretty sure the enemy will be meeting us in this full on exchange. Small vessels won't have anything to contribute."

"We are at extreme range," Redding announced. "Enemy has opened fire."

"Hold fast," Gray said. "They can't do any appreciable damage yet. They're just trying to make us flinch."

Pulse blasts glanced past them, disappearing into the ether. Those few which connected with their shields were absorbed harmlessly, barely causing a tremor as the Behemoth plodded along, racing toward their fate. The Tam'Dral kept pace with them, spreading out to give them some distance.

Clea leaned forward, clasping her hands in her lap as she watched the screen. Even if Protocol Seven didn't work on the Behemoth, it was installed and prepped on the Tam'Dral. And while they may not have the same advantage, their weapons still *hurt* the enemy defenses. Their part of the fight would remain conventional but effective.

I have faith in Lieutenant Darnell. He wouldn't have sent this algorithm if he didn't believe in it.

"Protocol Seven ninety-two percent installed," Paul announced.

"Enemy moving into optimal range, sir." Tim made the comment. He leaned back in his seat and stared at his own console as if something might leap out and grab him at any moment. Redding's left hand poised over weapon control, her other operating their maneuvering thrusters. Tension in the bridge made it clear the real fighting was about to begin.

"Let's give them a false sense of hope," Gray said. "Redding, turn and give them half a broadside. I want the weapons recharged when Protocol Seven is ready."

"Aye, sir."

Gray leaned toward his com to speak to the Tam'Dral. "Do *not* fire until we give the order. I want this to be a real surprise for our friends so I'm going to let them think we're still all operating under the same rules."

Clea sat up straighter. "You mean to show them their men were successful in killing the patient, if indeed that's why they were there."

Gray shrugged. "Why not? It may give them the confidence to go back on their wild offensive they seem to like so much."

"Which would lead them right into a blast of fire their defenses won't stop," Everly smiled. "Good idea, sir."

"Let's not count the explosions before the shots are fired," Gray replied.

The Behemoth pivoted, moving away from the Tam'Dral so they opened their port side to the enemy. Redding swiped up with her left hand and tapped something at the top. Half their weapons engaged, pulse blasts ripping through vacuum toward their intended targets. A number of direct hits flashed against shields, harmlessly absorbed.

"Direct hits," Paul said. "Damage to shields, as expected. Their power reserve dropped to eighty-five percent but is already recharging."

Tim squinted. "They're picking up speed!"

"Looks like your ploy may have worked." Clea fought not to tap her foot nervously. A bead of sweat formed on the side of her head which she did her best to ignore. Never before had she been so anxious to see a result. It wasn't fear but something else driving her emotions. *Perhaps I'm allowing myself a lot of hope. If this works, my people may be saved.*

"Enemy is engaging on both fronts," Paul said. "They are attacking the Tam'Dral *and* us, sir...they also seem to be charging."

"Where're you with my install?" Gray nearly growled. Clearly, his patience ran thin and his military side showed. He wanted to end this as much as Clea did but perhaps more so.

"Ninety-nine percent!" Paul seemed ready to burst with emotion. "Why the hell does it always stop at ninety-nine percent!?"

"Tam'Dral, this is Captain Atwell." Gray gripped his arm rests until his knuckles turned white. "Prepare to fire on my command. With or without us, use the protocol seven algorithm and tear these bastards apart. Do you copy?"

"This is Lieutenant Oxton, sir," a woman's voice replied over the spakers. "I copy. We have weapons lock and are ready to engage. Protocol Seven is ready."

A blast from the enemy shook the Behemoth, jostling Clea in her seat. She wanted to rush over to Paul's console again to see where he was at but she refrained, fighting to remain seated. She'd helped as much as she could. The fight, everything happening at that moment, sat squarely on the shoulders of others. Playing the role of observer never felt so frustrating.

"Shields holding," Paul said. "Power fluctuation on deck three…mess area."

"At least the ice cream will stay cold," Redding muttered, drawing a laugh from Tim. The brief moment of levity seemed to cut the tension, if only for a moment. Gray started tapping his knee.

"Paul, you'd damn well better have some good news!"

The enemy started to press into short range and another blast shook the ship. The Tam'Dral took a similar pounding. Time was absolutely running out.

Every shot they allowed their opponents to take held a chaotic potential, to take out shields, their weapons or even get lucky enough to blow their pulse core.

"We are now within close range!" Redding stiffened. "Permission to fire at will?"

"Paul!" Gray shouted.

"It's installed! It's installed!" Paul bounced in his seat. "Gathering shield readings...inputting to the weapons console...five seconds...three...now! It's ready now, sir! Now! Fire!"

"Tam'Dral, open fire!" Gray gestured to Redding. "Coordinate the assault! Shoot!"

Redding slammed her hand into the console, tapping away furiously as their weapons discharged. Clea held her breath as the pulse blasts raced toward their targets. A moment passed...they saw the Tam'Dral light up, their own weapons lancing through the darkness. *Will this work?*

No green flash emitted from around the enemy, no indication of shields at all. Just massive bouts of bulbous fire erupting from the metal as the ships were torn into. Large chunks of hull were torn free and though they tried to perform evasive maneuvers, it was far too late. They were in the kill box.

The Behemoth obliterated the one on the left, leveraging blast after blast upon them until their engines stopped and they began to drift. The Tam'Dral showed similar luck though their opponent put up a fight to the bitter end. An exchange of fire ended when several weapons on their opponent's vessel exploded, allowing bouts of flame to escape for several moments before it went cold.

"Their shields were completely ineffective," Paul spoke solemnly. "Both ships are rapidly losing power."

"Now's our chance to take them," Clea said, "learn more from their technology, gather prisoners perhaps."

"Um…we might not have time," Paul replied. "Sir, I'm reading a massive energy build up from their core."

"Ruptured?" Gray asked.

"No, sir, this is definitely intentional."

Everly cursed. "A self destruct!"

"Give me a range of impact," Gray demanded. "What's minimum safe distance?"

"Two hundred thousand kilometers," Paul replied.

Clea closed her eyes. "How long before the explosion?"

"Two minutes."

"Can we get that far?" Gray asked Redding. "At full speed?"

"It would be close but...no, sir. I don't believe we can."

"We have another option." Clea stood. "Initiate the hyper jump. We can close that distance in a few seconds."

"That's a huge risk," Everly said. "If something goes wrong..."

Clea gestured at the screen. "Something *is* going wrong."

"Clea's right," Gray said. "Tam'Dral, do you have hyper jump capabilities?"

"No, sir but I know what you're asking. This ship is much faster than the Behemoth. We'll be out of the blast range in plenty of time. In fact, we're initiating thrusters now."

"Get out of here then." Gray turned to Tim. "I hope you've got a good set of navs for this."

"Aye, sir. I think I know just the place to get us to safety." Tim tapped away at his controls. "Course set and ready for your mark."

Gray hit his communicator. "Higgins, we're going to do a hyper jump."

"Is that a good idea?" Higgins asked. "We haven't tested it before."

"After taking out the two enemy ships, I got bored and thought why not try now?"

"We're ready for it down here. Go ahead."

Redding exchanged a glance with Tim and they began a countdown. Gray took Clea's arm and gestured for her seat. They both sat down and strapped in, leaning back. She had been in several hyper jumps before but never on an untested ship with an untested crew. The nerves in the room made her tremble.

This is not how I hoped to end my first mission with these people.

"Three..."

Clea watched Redding and Tim work in tandem, each entering in their consoles. Their voices betrayed their fear, even though they showed no other outward signs. These were serious professionals, despite their lack of advanced technological experience. After all, their actions may well destroy the entire ship. They carried such a heavy responsibility gracefully.

"Two..."

Gray reached over and patted her arm. He meant the gesture to be reassuring but she took it otherwise. He never would've shown concern in a physical manner, not if he didn't need the contact himself. If Captain Atwell was afraid, then he knew the possible consequences of what they were about to do. At least he didn't take it lightly.

"One..."

A mere second away from the largest step in human history: true faster than light travel. What a marvel...and a terrible reason for having to try it on such short notice.

The air crackled around her and the hull hummed with a low vibration. She watched the screen, adopting an impassive expression, one which betrayed far more than such a placid look might on a human being. She confined herself to hope but also, a sense of inevitability. Whatever took place, if they lived or died, they saved Earth and that meant a great deal.

"Engaging!" Redding shouted and hit a button.

Everything seemed to freeze around them. Sound, motion, sensation and even the air. A half a second of nonexistence settled over them like a heavy shroud of winter's snow. Clea saw it on Earth in the mountains. Great blankets of white, frozen water piled high. The sky and clouds stretched on forever, disappearing into a vast expanse of nothing.

The air in her lungs felt heavy then, as if she tried to breathe while submerged in the sea. Her eyes watered and skin tingled from the biting chill. Gray stood with her then, watching as she smiled at the sensations washing over her. The two of them had been friends for over a year during that trip and he promised to show her something new.

All these thoughts drifted in and out of her mind before a painful rush of existence descended upon her. Computers beeped, the hull groaned and gasps of shock erupted all around her. The suddenness of it all hurt her ears and she leaned forward, rubbing her eyes with the heels of her hands. People spoke around her but she couldn't understand the words.

We survived.

"We made it!" Tim's voice was the first she made out and he hooted with excitement. "We're barely ten kilometers off our target! Way to go, Redding!"

"Couldn't have done it without you, partner. Good work!"

Gray stood from his chair and stretched before stepping forward. "Everyone, excellent work." He tapped something on Paul's console and they saw the enemy vessels on the screen. Hardly five seconds passed before they both exploded in two spectacular green orbs. Everyone looked away as the light faded, leaving behind empty space and debris.

"Excellent work, sir." Everly approached Gray and shook his hand. "You handed the enemy their asses here today."

"Only sort of," Gray replied. "We had a lot of help and some good fortune. The loss of those ships is going to be painful but at least we came away with something. Bodies from the invasion for one, the Tam'Dral for another and all that debris we might be able to salvage something from."

"We'll have to get crews out here before it drifts too far," Everly said. "I'll work with Ensign White to coordinate it."

"Get the Tam'Dral on coms as well." Gray returned to his seat. "We've got some people to bring aboard and a whole crew to revive. I think it's high time those people get on with their lives." He turned to Clea. "How're you doing there?"

"Your hyper jump test was quite successful."

Gray grinned. "Vague answer to my question. You look moved."

"Did you feel anything during the jump?" Clea asked. "Anything at all?"

"Truth be told, I don't hardly remember it." Gray shrugged. "What about you?"

"I...was back on the mountain during our leave time, do you remember?"

"Like...you had a vision of it?"

Clea nodded. "Sort of. I remembered the feeling on my skin and lungs, the view...Not the smell, though. Just the rest. Then we were back here. I've never had such a sensation during a hyper jump before."

"We do it special here on Earth?" Gray joked but his expression sobered. "Maybe you should visit the medical bay. Or maybe you're just exhausted. It's been a long day."

Clea nodded. "It has...full of emotion and stress, I agree. But I'm sure I'm fine. I'll see the rest of this through before I head to my quarters."

"Very good." Gray turned away. "Tim, set us a course for home and have the Tam'Dral rendezvous there. Redding, full speed once you have a heading. Then I want you all to take your relief. This was the busiest shift of our lives and you all deserve some downtime. Thank you again for a job well done."

Clea sat back in her seat and let herself relax. She felt honored to be part of their crew, to sit amongst them in their moment of triumph. They struggled, lost and won a great deal that day. Their species knew they stood a chance, proved to themselves their capability to survive in the larger, galactic theater. This point in history would be remembered for lifetimes to come and Clea along with it.

Finally, she knew she'd done her family name proud.

Epilogue

Gray reported to Earth command and gave them all the data they recovered. Doctors were dispatched to assist with the revival of the Tam'Dral crew. The shuttle which was used to penetrate the Behemoth hull was taken by technical crews to study and observe along with the bodies of the fallen. They would begin reverse engineering it all soon.

Clea prepared a dispatch for her people including everything they discovered. The Protocol Seven was not sent along but she alluded to it. They would need to come to Earth or vice versa to pass it along. Such information proved to be too valuable to risk it falling into enemy hands.

Salvage crews collected more rare materials from the combat zone than mining operations had managed in two years of constant work. Efforts toward building a second Behemoth were forwarded considerably and many of the roadblocks they faced were overcome. Instead of years, engineers believed they might have the ship operational in mere months.

Fatal casualties numbered low but a few good soldiers did not survive the engagement. Two of the marines died later from the intruder attack and several pilots also gave the ultimate sacrifice. Countless injuries would heal but many were effected by those they lost. Gray wrote letters to their families, condolences and explanations for how they served their people.

Olly and his crew received commendations for their work on the alien vessel. What they accomplished went well beyond anything anyone expected them to be capable of. They entered an unknown situation and wrangled it to their will through nothing short of genius work. All five of them became stars aboard the ship, at least for a little while.

Repairs to the Behemoth would not take long. Most of the work was to be done by Higgins own engineering crew. Most of the effort required environmental suits and time spent outside with pulse welding torches and new sheets of metal. Even so, they'd be combat operational inside three weeks, not a bad time frame considering all they'd been through.

Meagan Pointer received a commendation for her part in the conflict. Her wing, suffering the loss of one of their own, also received medals. The call went out for a new pilot to take Brian's place and they received over a hundred applicants. Everyone wanted in the hero wing and they all stood prepared to take their place amongst them.

Clea remained out of the spotlight, enjoying the successes of the others from afar. She read the tech briefs, watched the media outlets discuss their victory and quietly congratulated them individually. Whatever happened next, the Behemoth proved itself ready to fight. Her people placed their faith in the correct species, a once primitive group now proving their honor and nobility.

As she stood on the bridge of the Behemoth waiting for their orders, Gray nudged her arm as he came to stand beside her. She smiled at him, shoving him with her elbow. They stood in silence for several minutes before the Captain finally spoke, leaning so he might keep his voice down.

"You look just as somber today as you did back when we won the fight."

"Maybe that's just my resting face."

"Not when you beat me in chess," Gray replied. "I seem to recall every time that happens, you glow like your lottery numbers were called."

"Some victories are sweeter than others," Clea turned to him, admiring his face for a long moment. "Do you think of those we lost in the battle? The men and women who sacrificed their lives for the cause?"

Gray nodded. "Of course, I've never forgotten a single person I lost under my command. There's a weight to leadership not everyone's cut out for. If you can't live with what happens, you won't be successful."

"I wonder if I might have it in me to be the type of leader you are. To understand my responsibilities to such a profound degree and live with those decisions."

"You might have the chance to find out someday," Gray replied, "but you won't know until you try. If I was you and an opportunity presented itself, I'd take it. I know I'd follow you into battle any day of the week and twice on Sunday."

Clea rolled her eyes. "You're giving me a hard time."

Gray shook his head. "Not for a second."

"Everyone on this ship would follow you to the gates of hell themselves if they had to. What must that responsibility be like?"

"As long as you earn that trust, it's not a burden. And note, I'd have to be heading to the gates of hell for them to follow me. That's why they have my back. Because I won't ask any of them to do something I'm unwilling to do myself."

"Of course, like your Thermopylae example. King Leonidas leading his noble three hundred."

"With less attitude, I hope." Gray grinned. "Anyway, what's going on with all your heavy thoughts? Are you okay?"

Clea nodded. "I'm simply...self reflective, I suppose. Analyzing my own performance in the engagement."

"You helped Paul get Protocol Seven installed faster. If you'd done nothing else, I'd say you did your part."

"I appreciate that."

"You're welcome then." Gray motioned with his head. "Come on, I believe I have a chess match to win. It was my time, remember?"

Clea gave him a wide eyed, innocent look. "I was merely trying to spare your feelings."

Gray laughed. "Oh, we'll see about that."

He turned and left, Clea following slowly behind. She nodded her head, finally finding a smile. "Yes, I suppose we will."

55120400R00180

Made in the USA
San Bernardino, CA
28 October 2017